DOCTOR

—————— *of* ——————

SILENCE

fictions by

Robert Kelly

McPherson & Company

DOCTOR OF SILENCE

Library of Congress Cataloging-in-Publication Data

Kelly, Robert, 1935-
  Doctor of silence : fictions / Robert Kelly.
    p. cm.
  ISBN 0-914232-92-4 (alk. paper) : $20.00.
  ISBN 0-914232-91-6 (pbk.) : $10.00
    I. Title.
PS3561.E397D63   1988
813'.54—dc19   88-1624

ACKNOWLEDGMENTS
"The Woman with Five A's in Her Name" appeared first in *Fiction
International*. "Temple of Shiva" and "Hypnogeography" appeared first in
Notus. "A Line of Sight" was first published as a chapbook in the *Sparrow*
series of John and Barbara Martin's Black Sparrow Press, copyright © 1974 by
Robert Kelly.

CONTENTS

IV

V

Doctor of Silence

The alternate form (or allomorph) of any story is an animal. Any time you see an animal, be aware of narrative. It got here and is going somewhere else. The intersection we identify as "here," or "now," or "there is a rabbit on the lawn" is an episode in an immense and vertiginous history no one but we will ever read. But we usually look up from that page and drift away.

1

Pasatiempo

The sky is the color of pomegranates. The wall is white as a white wall in a sunny alley in California can be. We are near enough to personal salvation to smell it coming up from the hazy sea below the airport. Personal salvation tastes of Hawaii, or how we imagine that would be. We are talking to each other. We pick our syllables according to levels, and try to speak as few syllables as the sense will bear. Maybe there is so little sense we could just breathe.

There are the three of us. We count the syllables in each line. A transistor radio at the top of the steps in the shade of the stucco house-front painted lime is playing the last scene of *Der Rosenkavalier.* Arrangements are always being made, and sometimes our appointments are beautiful, beautiful commitments. But they are always arrangements, composites, unlasting. Would you even want them to last?

We decide languages slowly because we are disheartened. Nobody understands what the three women singing German are saying but it is sad, sad. The way everything is sad some days or some people always are. Always things ending or going away, and the dumb little smiles we put up with losses with, they just make everything sadder. How can you stand that music?

Lidia doesn't say. She sits sipping cold water on the broken patio. She has drunk two bottles of of Dos Equis and has eaten three bad burritos. She is drinking another bottle too, alternating sips, water, cerveza, and she is sad. She doesn't answer, and leaves it to Paco and Jim to work it out. I am Jim. I am not entitled to the name, though I come from a language where people can be named Jim. Paco is not entitled to his name either,

13

he doesn't even know Spanish, Lidia knows it better than either of us, and he isn't named Frank. Lidia tells us again that she heard once that in Mexico they have Tres Equis, really strong. We should go and see.

I can't stand that music, it's so sad. What do you expect, I ask him, it's German. He shakes his head and takes a bite of a cold cheese enchilada Lidia won't eat because it's made with Cheez Whiz. Paco doesn't drink beer or anything. I don't drink beer, I don't care how many x's the beer has. I am smoking and counting the walls I see around us. I am smoking and they are walls. Patio small knee-high whitewashed walls, small retaining wall to hold the lawn in, house walls, walls of other houses, two houses on this lot, walls of buildings across the street, walls of the pentecostal chapel with a dead green pickup parked two weeks in front of it, walls of a truck. Walls and weeks, I keep losing count. It's hard to decide just what constitutes a wall. Does a truck count? Does a little steeple widow's walk on the oldest house down the block fake new england qualify as four more walls around what is really only a ventilator housing full of slats or slots? It's so hard to count things, even to know whether they are actual things or not, or just part of other things. And those things, are they themselves, or just more parts?

In her left hand she has a jellyjar with Lake Arrowhead water in it from the big bottle standing on its head in the kitchen dispenser. In her right hand she has the seven-eighths full bottle of Dos Equis. The burrito lies between her sneakers right on the dirty step as if she was finished with it or doesn't care. The red evening sky makes green shadows. I call that to the attention of Lidia and Paco and they tell me, both of them, groaning, that I've told them that often before. Every time you sit out here at evening, she says. The ripples of the long weeds beside the dead fig tree ripple shadows a continuous green wave on a clean sidewalk. Everything changes at nighttime but not yet.

There is a lot of noise and Lidia looks up. Some liquid I'm not sure which dribbles around the knob of her chin and drips slowly along her long neck as she inspects the noise. A sad big DC 10 is coming in quietly above us towards its runway. It is coming from Hawaii I bet. I think I can hear under the quiet roar the clackety noise of the feeble wing ailerons being lifted to slow its descent.

There are three steps up from the street sidewalk to the broken patio in front of the house where I live with Lidia, and Paco comes to sponge on his sister. I sponge on her too in the sense that she gets a check every month from Jay her ex-husband, a neurologist in Fresno. I get not much from my activities as a sketch portrait artist in public parks and an astrological consultant in certain coffee houses in Venice. But I'm able to keep Lidia entertained with many drawings of her in her different moods and in different costumes some real some imagined. And I'm enough of an expert at astrology really to be able to warn her of unprofitable dope deals or inauspicious days for instance or tell her the ideal times to take to Brentwood boutiques the dried flower arrangements she makes sometimes.

I need a lot of sleep and this house isn't too quiet because of the airport and so on but I sleep deeply usually and sometimes I wake up and the house is empty and I like that fine. I can read a book or look at the ephemeris or just watch the snails nose along through the dichondra.

From the way Paco's fingers are tapping on his right knee, I can tell he's counting syllables. He's composing a poem, the kind that needs a certain number of syllables in every line. I don't like his poetry very much, but then I don't like any poetry very much. It seems to be a way of not saying anything, and I still have something to say. Maybe when I'm older I won't have anything to say, and then it will be fine to read poems.

When they catch the fox, do they kill him? Paco is wondering. Who? Foxhunters, the people on horses with red coats. No, I don't think they do. Of course they do, says Lidia, what would be the point if they didn't, how would they know they really caught him if he wasn't dead? He might have just stopped moving and let them find him standing there. Why are you worried about foxes, I want to know, and then I know it's a dumb question, because I saw his fingers counting, and I know he's in a poem, and poems are places where nothing seems to be irrelevant or especially stupid, so why not foxes. But he answers me anyhow: I was just just wondering. I like foxes.

The Tower

He first began to think he might be running a fever when he
stopped halfway up the trail to piss in the shelter of a hornbeam
glistery from the recent rain. The fine mid-morning stream of
his urine hissed into the delve between two exposed roots just
where they left the trunk. Steam rose up. It puzzled him, since
the day was mild, soft, not a hint of chill in the air, though not
warm either—a day you could call tepid if you were being disa-
greeable. He wasn't, not at all; he was happy with the morning
and the silent woods, nobody bothering him. Why would the
urine smoke that way? Ninety-eight point six degrees, was it,
why should that smoke, like the thin lacquer-colored stream
from the teapot, good strong tea. Why now, when the thermom-
eter was probably close to seventy, would that little difference
matter? Would the difference steam? But maybe he had a fever.
Then the urine would be warmer than normal, wouldn't it. It
does work that way, he thought, body temperature. If higher,
then body fluids warmer. How warm? Same as rest of body?
Suppose a fever of 104 degrees—would that account for the
steam rising? It might, especially considering that the fever
would make him feel the day's weather warmer than it actually
is. His body temperature is say, 104, and the weather outside
might be then five or ten degrees cooler, actually, the way we
measure, how could he be sure. It might be 55 here under the
dank trees, a good fifty degrees difference then between the air
and the fluid. It isn't certain.

By now he had reached the place where the path divides—north to the lower woods, or west, the track that coiled
gently, ever rising, to the highest point, on which, he had been

told, a fire-tower stood. It could not be, he thought, a very successful tower, since he had never seen it from down below, as often as he had walked around the edges of the woods. He chose the tower walk, with its hint of something man-made, maybe ancient, in the middle of this calm natural. Before him the path was pleasant to walk on under so many leaves, maple and sumac and ash, not mucky yet with too much rain as it would be in November. Damp below the leaves, dry on their surfaces—good traction, good cushioning both. A nice walk. Traces of deer and raccoon, and horse-droppings too, just once on the whole length of the trail. The rider must have cut through one of the more open woodlots. Only the deer spoor seemed recent. He had come in sight of the tower even before he could feel nervous about finding it. There it was, off to the left, only a few hundred feet further on the path that was beginning to wind in more tightly now as it reached its goal, the top of what must be the highest hilltop here.

The tower was made of wood, new wood, still pale from the hands of the carpenters, and the bolts that held beam to cross-piece, rungs to uprights, were still shiny. Men like towers. They are tall and upright, confidently assertive without much fuss, phallic, conspicuous. Above all, they have the reputation of being both useful and symbolic. The men who built this must have left the hill proud of their work, the good pressure-treated lumber, the tight fit. Not even a creak of wood as he set foot on the first rung. The two levels of the tower were reached by ladders. The first had the slats of its rungs set flat side up, more like steep stairs. Climbing this brought him to a platform twelve feet above the hilltop; a swinging gate gave him entrance to the platform which he crossed to reach the second ladder, this one steeper, its rungs mounted edgewise up. He held tight and mounted cautiously, and found himself about twenty feet above the hilltop. Off west there might be the luminosity of the river, or it might just be sky. Otherwise, this curious tower was not higher than the reddening treetops that surrounded it. He was above the earth but could see nothing of it.

In one intact sudden clutch of feeling, right in the core of a slight shortness of breath from the climb, he felt moved by an impulse of generosity, strange after the emotionally arid hours of his day so far, strange, yet safe too, since what did he have to give, and to whom could he give it? He wanted to bless this earth and its trees and animals and insects, the stripy chipmunks and the anxious fox, but had nothing to bless them with. He stood a few minutes at each of the four edges of the platform, vaguely, without discipline, trying to resurrect in himself some worship of directions, elements, the teeming proliferation of mind, stories, wishes, hopes. All he could feel, really, though, was anxiety about the unrailed edge, the pale wood of the steps, the awkwardness of the descent. He came down.

Near the base of the tower was a shapely pile of worked stones that were surely the base of some building of long ago, perhaps an earlier tower, stone, or based on stone. The way the stones had fallen left gaps and crevices, small steps and deep little caverns. He wanted to step up the wet earth, bare here, that led between the two halves of the fallen structure. On a hilltop, even a foundation can fall.

He knew it would be full of snakes—they love this kind of ruin, lots of grooves and slots for them and their loved ones, the den. The thought of snakes, in their numbers, kept him from walking up onto the pile of rocks. Yet he wanted to bless the snakes. Who am I to bless anything? he thought. He remembered the poem of Coleridge, he was sure, where the mariner blessed the snakes. What were the snakes doing in the ocean, though? Was it a metaphor?

If I want to bless the snakes, he thought, I would have to be someone who can bless things—a god, for instance. What would it feel like to be a god? He half-closed his eyes and imagined himself looking out of god eyes at the snake-infested mound, he imagined his eyes glowing with love and blessing, and willing his god will to carry that love out of his eyes into the crannies of the rocks, where they waited, perhaps even looking forward to his blessing, perhaps even aware of it and him in some way. How can we know, he wondered.

I don't know whether I blessed them or not, I don't know if anything has changed. He thought that way as he walked down the hill, forgetting snakes and tower, just watching his step. For a moment, the woods ahead of him and below him had the look of a huge face seen very close up, like the eyebrow and eye and nose of a lover beside you on a pillow. Then that appearance was gone and the woods were just themselves, and a late autumn mosquito drifted by like a thought in the mind of this god.

The Island

There was a time when things kept coming towards me and I let them. Then there was a month when the moon fell away from anything I wanted to say about it, shy, shy. Then after that the sun gave me some trouble with its anxiety to reach that part of the galaxy we fancifully describe to ourselves as the haunches of Sagittarius. And where is that going, in turn, who knows. So I decided to go to an island, next best thing to a woman. Why not a woman, you ask? Past all metaphor, there is a person. I am not always, one is not always, worthy of another person's person-hood (as therapists who wear turquoise and silver bolo string-ties on their tattersall shirts like to call it). Not enough to say Woman, woman. An island lets you do what you want, within reason, though reason is seldom on the mind, at least the mind of those who choose to go to islands. Later I may have some-thing to say about the color of her hair, and how she looks back over her shoulder as she walks away and catches me staring at her supple rump, and other things that justify the ways of God to man. Probably not. But right now it is enough to choose the island, not her. Not herself, *l'isola,* and that's enough.

My ankles were still wet, therefore still accumulating grains of sand as I trudged up the beach. The dory slapped up and down in the mild swell of the surf, kept in place more or less by the hawser tied to the oarlock tied to the cinderblock tossed with a grunt (mine) to the pile of rocks I'd aimed at all the way in through the bay. It is so boring, bor-ing, wanting the same person year after year, the sway of the same supple conditions through the dingy alleys of the head, the only clean thing there the walkways polished smooth by their passage. Her passage. What was I doing here? Trying to follow.

When you want someone enough they become an island. They lose all connection to the people around them and exist for you in a fabulous remoteness, but one you can swim or paddle to, taking years to get there, and land furtively on their unguarded shores. Think like this long enough and one day you find yourself barefoot in wet sand, trudging towards some misty you suppose they must be palm trees they look so like cartoons of desert islands and one turns to the other and says, What do you say? Dear Heart, I have come to your island.

Underfoot, the anonymous coral rubbish and silicaceous treasure-house of unappreciated differences (my powerful metaphor for sand) gives way to something less slidey-slidey, something cooler, and I'm walking on common earth, even some grass on it to cool and confuse me, it's not a park, it's a coral atoll, a treasure island. Don't confuse me. I heard a sound like the surf suddenly accelerated by an insane conductor, like one of those nut passages in Rossini where everybody sings as fast as they can but still can't keep up with the orchestra in the pit, which is unfair since the orchestra first of all has nothing to say except music, and music is never particular, and secondly the players don't have to wear makeup and peculiar costumes ill-suited to their frames. Nobody can see where the music is coming from. But I could. I had reached the top of a little knoll (what is a knoll? how different from a knop? a rise? a kopje? a ridge? a hillock?) and all around me were these ragged trunks and spiny barked trees, their huge dead leaves lying around their bases along with all sorts of other trash. Organic. When I looked up I could see the beautiful green big fans swaying, palm trees indeed. And ahead of me, through the trees, a downslope leading to the source of the noise: a four-lane highway, light traffic, just now a behemoth on six axles was doing its Doppler Effect, and the back-roar came to me mingled with the alto whine of a sort of Maserati clipping along in the other direction. The big truck had OXOX painted in blue eight foot letters across its rear double doors. I took it as a good sign, and read it out loud as Hugs and Kisses, Hugs and Kisses, although when I first saw this grapheme at the foot of a girlish letter (fortunately addressed to me) I took the O as a lewder invitation.

So this is your island, this is the kind of girl you are. There were so many things I had been worrying about I forgot all about fantasizing what you'd actually be like. I kept thinking about what you looked like, how you smelled, the sound of your voice as you whispered some nonsense you'd read in a book into my actual ear the night we first met sixty thousand years ago, the sound of that voice still coupled with the smell of your young mouth and my painful memories of your pale pink lips moving, enjoying the words you were specifying. I remember everything but the words, which goes to show you something. But what my mind was full of about you has always been its own take, it's busy with its own perceptions and its memories of them, not of you, the mind is busy with itself. And here you were, I mean here you are, palm trees, sexy beaches, zephyrs, sportscars zooming by, traffic keeping to the left, and over there an actual flag, blue bunting, the double cross of your mother island's apt symbolism.

Wait a minute, wait just one minute now. I'm beginning to sound like an angry lover, a certain resentment (what does *ras-sentiment* really mean?) has crept out of my mouth like the viper in what's his name's allegorical painting of Envy. Or was it Anger? I'm too old to believe in Existenz, all I have is going on. And you have been one of the more tolerable goals my fancy has tormented itself with over the last years. There have been times I thought you were a voice from heaven.

She does not love me. That song finally came clear one day, and after I got tired of singing it to different tunes in different registers, tired of eye-carving its runes on the bleak streets of my neighborhood, bleak with herlessness, I mean, I mean I just got tired of, I suppose you could call it, the pain. Tired of pain, tired of song, what does a body do then? Subtly I had turned from her lover to her invigilator (a fancy word to mean I scrutinize every choice she makes) to her invader. Me now, landing on her shores. Her flanks. Again, what am I doing here? Is this rape? How could it be? Rape needs resistance. Needs force. Not this stumbling ashore in wet pants unopposed. Her shrine, her wine-land, her whoosh of traffic, her Kimberly, her General Mines. Was I supposed to find her treasure? Or was I a vagabond

semi-precious stone ready for her to find, to pick up and slip in
her snug pocket? That image would be sexy for a while, until the
inconvenience of my imprisonment outweighed the ardent fancies of an ex-lover suddenly intimate with his not-so-long-ago
obsession.

No, the only resistance here is mine. Me. Trying to be an
ex-lover in the middle of a caper that made sense only for a
hopeful swain. I sat down on one of the tree-stump posts they
used to support the rustic-effect railing along this side, not the
other side, of the motorway. Think about this, don't just put one
foot after the other as usual marching down into the valley of
the shadow of Desire, think now, nobody has seen you, you
haven't declared anything or broken anything, except your own
resolutions maybe, just go back to the boat, what did I call it,
dory, back to that and row away. Now. Do it.

No. I wanted to see her, or, if this island was her, I wanted
to get to know it. Walk all over it, get the feel of the place, other
transparent metaphors for an intimacy that is, after all, not such
a big deal. Everybody in the world does it, even me, why am I
making such a fuss about this woman, by no means the only
one, not even for me, special, yes, but how special you do need
her to be, O Mind, O Great Hairy Romantic Mind, O Great
Hairy Romantic Self-Regarding Self-Involved Self-Protecting
Mind o' Mine? Etc.

No good. I wanted to be here and I was staying. Shut up, I
said to myself, leave it alone. Here we are and here we're going
to stay. To prove it, I got up and started walking along the road,
in the direction from which the sportscar had been coming—
either smart people lived that way, or there was some attraction
that drew them thither. A moment later, I realized the same
logic could support the other direction as well, but I was off at
last. The sun was busy setting to my right—the kind of meaningless detail I can't help thinking about, but that just makes
everything harder to understand, just one more thing to remember, but there it was, bothering the palm trees and agaves with a
light pinkish from the haze of smog in which it sank. No cars
were coming towards me, but several overtook me on the other
side of the road. All of them were recent poshnesses of Euro-

provenience, all piloted by young women. What could I have expected? Who else was here but herself? But wouldn't I also find here the male projections of her mind, those tedious louts and oafish cock-waddlers whose real-world semblances I had often enough seen her dancing with and getting married to? How boring for me if this island turned out to be her zoo, her stud-farm, or the tropic breeding ground of the mental arche-types from which she stocked it. Trapped on an island of other men! Boychiks and torpedos pullulating all round me, gaping gossoons and zit-crazed wankers, thin-mustached tenors and palsied tycoons, actors and monsignors and the mailman, Mr Fixit and the Count of Monte Cristo, a lone centerfielder staring into the deceptive sun. It did not bear thinking about. I took comfort from the sex of the passing motorists, which remained feminine.

This was a congenial road, level, warm, not so many trucks. No one had stopped to offer me a lift, but nothing in my bearing suggested I needed one. I just kept walking, happy enough not to have to explain anything to anybody. People who do you favors always have a lot to say. And to ask. It was one of those mo-ments where I had a little difficulty remembering my name (Don Ernesto? Herr Gnadenvoll? The Duke of Mantua? some-thing like that), at least when pressed by distaff interlocutors. The sun was going down and I was getting nowhere and I was happy, and so on and so on, but even so, I ought to know *some-thing* about what I was up to. Even in opera the characters use words, I suppose, that have some kind of meaning. Remarks to make whilst being entombed beneath the level of the Nile. What to say just before leaping off parapets into the Tiber. Not much field of application, yet there is *some* meaning. And that's how I learned to talk, pithy comments of frightening overspeci-ficity. But could I say what I was doing on this dewy island? Nah. (I mean the ordinary Brooklyn sound pronounced [nae:], with faint prenasalization. It is strange there is no dictionary way to write it.) And dewy it was as it darkled, darkled and cooled down. Wise in the ways of the world, I began to sing.

A car was slowing behind me, strolling beside me, its sleek snout stopping a few paces in front of me so its driver could look up at me from her low coachwork and leather and inspect whatever it is that women see when they look at men.

"Get in," she said. A certain lilt in her voice made it sound a little like a question, a little like that special West Coast way women have of making a statement sound like a question. Fragments of a demure age, last shreds of wholesome insecurity?

I crossed in front of the car, taking my time, and climbed in beside her, not all that easy with my long legs and clown feet, and smiled at her. "Is this trip necessary?" I asked, to keep my self-respect. Then realized I'd lost it by a piece of dated whimsy that only made me older, her younger.

The car had shown its breeding, shooting up the road an eighth of a mile by the time she answered, if answer it was: something about illegal aliens, pity, cold night, last act of some opera, I reminded her of her brother or her sister's husband I couldn't be sure and didn't care, did I know it was Christmas Eve? I explained that I thought palm trees and coral atolls canceled out Christmas, that surely this earthly paradise was post-Christian, or at least pre-Christian, as technically it should be, should have been, it's Christ OR California, baby.

When women sing together, it is the stars. When men hear this singing, it means something is ready to be born—she had things of this sort to say, things I deemed strictly coo-coo, but with a pleasant resonance, as if muffled reverberations of some ancient and reasonable understanding long ago shattered into inept occultries. I went along with her mood enough to flourish a few classic examples of what I thought she was talking about, Sirens and Ulysses, Sibyl and Aeneas, same Sibyl a good many years later *mise en bouteille* and complaining in Greek to some yuppie youths from a callow culture just about to make its mark.

"Have you finished?" she wanted to know. Before I had chance to decide one way or the other, she launched into an analysis of someone who could only be me, an ingrate and alien and interloper and intruder, a man (at least that) of coarse humor and all too finite jest, with big feet. She had noticed, and I found her inclusion of these pedal enormities (paraphrase, not quotation) of mine quite endearing. "You noticed!" I said, and reached

over, snaking my hand around the stickshift erect in its leather
volcano-bag and laying it tenderly in her lap.

There is a hiddenness in things, in us all. We do and do not
know, we do and don't do, it happens and we forget and it
happens again. It means all right, but we lose our grip on its
meaning and it slips away and the sea comes back, the moon
falls up again and there you are. She stopped the car and got out,
abruptly. My hand fell onto the leather seat warm from her. I
didn't know what she was doing, my caress had not been menacing enough for flight to be appropriate, not erotic enough for her
to be so swiftly compliant. What was she doing? She had come
around to my side, and pulled my door open, pulled my arm
hard. I got out, expecting to be jettisoned and left on the road. I
was resigning myself to this (I am a great resigner): a few miles
further I'd come, and it was not much darker. And certainly not
colder.

But she closed the door and took my arm, firmly, and with a
faint trace of something that might even be courtesy led me off
onto the grassy verge and up a little hill. Quickly, so quickly, I
allowed myself to be taken in hand, allowed her to establish the
terrain we moved on, the rules, the domain, the religion we were
to worship in. It is as it has always been with me, conforming
myself to their universe, her universe. I walked in the dark and
she led me. I resented this compliance in me and tried to bring
some news of my resentment to my mouth in the form of words
of moderated, cultivated, even interesting anger. But everything
I could think of felt swinish and small.

We were climbing in the almost dark, and this hill did not
have much in the way of trees on it, though there were agaves or
things shaped like them that hacked at my legs as I passed. I
wondered if her island ran to snakes and scorpions, and the
funny way I found to ask about them was this: "Is there anything to be afraid of?" The hand that held my arm let go, and the
whole of her arm came round my back and squeezed me; I
experienced a humiliating comfort, reassurance. "You have been
here before, but you forgot. You always forget. Sometimes you
think it is an island, sometimes a city or a book you can't seem
to get the hang of, or a movie you fall asleep in the middle of and

wake to find the movie over, the theater empty, cold wind shuf-
fling the candy wrappers around your ankles. There, do you see
it?"

She was pointing straight ahead of us, where the sea ought
to be if my sense of direction was working. What I saw was
uneasy dark huddled movements with glints and sighings in it.
"The sea," I said.

"That's all you are, and all you have. Go, make sense of it!"

Before I had a chance to discuss the matter, she had shoved
me forward hard, just where the slope began to fall. I was unpre-
pared (as usual) and couldn't keep my footing. I tried hurrying
forward to catch up with my feet but they kept slipping down
what could only be sand and pebble, then suddenly not even
that, and I was sliding on my side down something more like a
lazy cliff than a steep hill. The mind has a velocity of its own,
and was busy with several anxieties not altogether germane to
my swiftly-changing situations as I fell, most of them about
drowning, and lust, and the identity of the woman, or were they
women, who had just shoved me to my death or whatever this
was coming, and not least about the remembered feel of warm
leather on my hand. Splashdown in tidal pool. No deaths, no
breaks. Bone-whole I rose, soaked and almost amused. When I
looked back up the slope I could see her outlined against the sky.
It seemed only fitting to wave a friendly farewell. If it was a
farewell. I mean, how was I going to go anywhere? Be reasonable. Boatless, mapless, lightless. I reflected upon women, upon
Delilah for example, until the image of me as a dazzled Samson
made me laugh out loud.

"What's so funny," she called down from her serene high-
ness. I determined to keep her wondering, and set out sloshing
my way along the shore, in the direction I supposed we had
come from, that would lead me to my boat, sooner or later. Or
some other vessel. We have our pride too.

The Dash Across the Border

He had been preparing for years. The room itself was stripped down to the essential instruments and techniques. On the darkest wall large oblongs of more vivid yellow showed where bookshelves had been taken away. Their contents painfully memorized, memorialized, dispersed, concentrated, he had given away along with the cases themselves. Through the compliance or indifference of the landlord (a man silent and friendly enough to accommodate either interpretation) he had been allowed successively to brick up several windows of the room, leaving only the one that pointed in his proper direction. Uncurtained, this one gave upon the salt marsh and, far off to the left, a glimpse of the dull metal cage-work of the bascule bridge that one day had brought him to this coastal almost-island. The window faced north-northeast, and what light he had came reasonably steady.

Several years before, he had eliminated from the room all the technology of eating. His daily meal he took at a businessmen's café in the district. He would approach its low-ceilinged dining room shortly after sunset, and spend an hour or more relishing his dinner; he was not above talking to some acquaintance who by chance or design had sat down nearby. However freely he may have conversed, he would always leave alone, if necessary dismissing his companion on the sidewalk in front of the café with civility. He would return to his own room by choosing one from a set of circuitous routes he had defined, all of which shared the final and penultimate phases: a walk along the beach, and then up the Rua Augustin in the direction of the marsh as far as the door of his own house. Upstairs, in the room, not even an empty glass bore witness to his capacity, which we all share, for transforming animals and vegetables into flesh and feeling. If he was thirsty, he would bend and drink from the bathroom tap, like a deer perhaps from a reliable spring in an obscure reach of the rainforest.

Mornings, not necessarily soon after he rose, he would at some point leave the room and carefully reverse the route he'd taken the evening before. This symmetry meant to lay a syntactic embrace around the nighttime, and establish continuity of consciousness through the dark. This morning walk may well have been brisker than the after-dinner stroll—and what harm in that? In speaking carefully a remark of some importance, one may approach slowly the pivot or high pass of the sentence then, the crisis surmounted, the thing said, hurry along to the conspicuous, even inevitable, end. So the now familiar walk would bring him quickly, his pace helped along by an appetite we all share, morning, dinner a thing of the past, the wind meeting us, the seashell of the mouth full of salts and tides. Soon he would be again at the doorway of the café. Once there, he would lay a hand on the young elm tree, already pollarded, that had grown up from the square meter of earth allowed it at the sidewalk's edge. His hands in contact with the tree, he'd look up into the sky, and then enter the intersection, broad enough to be called a square or plaza, though it wasn't, to another café catercorner to his dinner of the night before. In this, his morning restaurant, he would have his thick coffee, study the paper, and receive and often read his mail, delivered there and kept for him. He had no wish to receive mail or messages at his room, yet knew it wrong and discourteous to deny others all access to his attention. The proprietor of the café extended the convenience to him without charge, out of a general humankindness not rare in his profession, and to be of service to what was, after all, seven days a week year in and year out, a most regular customer. It is true that his purchases were few, but he made a good breakfast, and tipped the owner's none too bright niece appropriately. Since this café did not serve an evening meal, he could without the least disloyalty or infidelity dine every night at O Camafeu (itself not open for breakfast), and take coffee and rolls with his mail every morning at O Cervo Loiro.

Three cups of coffee drunk, the paper read, the mail read

and usually discarded unanswered, sometimes with some mail in his pocket too, for interesting reports and recitals did come to him now and then, he would set out on the walk home.

Now this walk was the chief muscular enterprise of the day. He could, if he liked, walk unconsciously, since this walk, unlike the evening one, did not have to be repeated, retrograde, the following day. In fact, by his law, it could not be repeated on any given day. This was the freedom walk, and he set great value on it—it was his belief that one day this very walk, or one free walk like it, might itself lead him across the border.

What made him think there *is* a border, an other side? He had asked himself and answered himself scores of times, from the very first days of his planning. The testimony of men. Men before him, from the earliest times of record, had set down in language and emblem news of the border, their own attempts, the sudden disappearances of their colleagues, the quick raptures that survivors would find swelling inside them in the hour of the vanishing of their friends, words spoken in their inner ears, names called out triumphantly in the dark. The word was out.

Reading and research, and more than those, his long conversations with other exiles, had convinced him that there were two ways of crossing the border. One is an unconscious sweet sleep or sleep-walking from which one awakened to find oneself *over there,* and the other a deliberate most certainly conscious plunge through rarely manifested conditions, alignments of one's own energies with the constantly and significantly shifting structures of the world. The first way was simple, the second so difficult some doubted it could be done at all. Neither was sure of accomplishment. The simple way might just not ever happen. The hard way might fail every time, or every apparent time. So much had to be known all at one time—not as bits of data, but as actual, real-time embraces of knowing and things known.

He thought of these two ways, by a pardonable metaphor, as outer and inner, and, by a whimsical extension of the metaphor, as the Way of the Street and the Way of the Room.

Now this noontime walk, and it so often coincided with noon though his law did not require it to do so, would take him along the streets of his quarter, under grey skies, slowly, dreamingly, past houses where old women sat at windowsills on which tame birds were airing in their little bamboo cages, past front yards where gaudy white calla lilies untended stretched up above unmown salty rough grasses, past corner groceries where two young women, one entering empty-handed, one leaving with her purplish net-bag full of bread and smoked meats already making their white wrapping paper oily translucent like the sky just before dark, might meet and stand in uncommitted talk while he walked by. On the two concrete steps up to the grocery they might stand, or one with a foot to the sidewalk and a foot on the first step, rhythmically or almost rhythmically might sway forward and back from the waist as it seemed, though really only the lower foot was moving, unseen architect of her interesting motion, heel to ball, foot shifting her not considerable weight, ball to heel. He found it interesting, at any rate, to watch this empty-handed woman move almost as if some other were moving her, while she talked of that and this from her soft mouth. Very much she'd talk from her mouth, fronting the words, while the other woman would stand firmer, perhaps easing the weight of her shopping bag by propping it between the doorpost and her hip. He found it interesting, angles, curves, and his pace discernibly slowed as he approached them. For it was in such presentments of the fact of the world, such instant, undiscourseful manifestations of its suchness, that he hoped he might be plunged, by his natural interest (spontaneous movement of the mind) and never wake again until his abstracted thought had been carried by his automaton of a no less abstracted body, all by itself! to the other side. And then he would be there. There, thanks to a locked parrot or a faded hedge or a couple of housewives talking in their soft mouths.

This free walk every noon time had, like any freedom, rules of its own. The neighborhood in which he lived and walked was not large, a settlement on what had once been a sort of island linked at low tide to the mainland, and now linked all day long to the more important suburbs off south and west. This almost-island had once been fancied as a summer place, and some few more venturous immigrant contractors had summoned forth a few dozen little streets of beach houses, a few squares, two avenues running the length of the island (as it was now to be called), and one prospect. But the marsh had been no one's idea of a thing to look at, and bred eight months of the year insect vectors of several by now rather old-fashioned diseases. Landfill stopped. Development stopped. Civil engineering was difficult, bureaucratic decisions easy and arrived at far away, so the marsh remained as it was. The more respectable sorts of poor people were permitted to move in all year round. The beach houses became houses. The prospect became an ordinary avenue, peculiar only in having houses on one side and swamp on the other, swamp and sea, you can do nothing with the sea; the developers had given up before the stage was reached where royal palms would have to be planted along the wide road. The houses here looked at the sea unimpeded, and a fine view could be had of the marsh itself where children played loudly and stranger adults built campfires and killed rats and huddled together in the gloaming. Beyond the marsh people could see the city whose clients they had become. This then was the whole district, from end to end perhaps half a mile, two avenues deep, not counting the prospect. Above the highest widow-walks and chimneys, and higher even than the twin steeples of the neo-colonial church, the tower of the bascule bridge stood in the sky, patron of the whole enterprise. From his window, he could see part of this bridge.

His room was in a house on the prospect, and his cafés were on the further of the two avenues. So the rule by which he directed his free walk allowed him to stroll, however indirectly, only towards the sea or marsh. Under no circumstances, then, might he approach the bridge, or even walk towards the mainland. This was not superstition, of course, since every morning and evening he had to move exactly towards just this bridge and just that mainland, by the mere fact of stepping towards his cafés. It was not after all a matter of direction as such, but the fit of circumstances themselves. Few things have any meaning out of context, and least of them, perhaps, the petals of the compass. His freedom walk, if one day it should happen to succeed, must take him out, away from land and city. He honored that ever-present possibility, or the possibility of that possibility, by the scrupulous navigation wherewith he set himself to dream his way, each day around noon, back to his room.

The walk had another peculiarity, one the reader may already have divined. He was to notice things. He was to keep on the lookout for sensible objects, persons, relations, any one of which might be right for his ultimate single purpose. To have one purpose! Would it dream him along? So as he walked, he tested everything he saw by the touchstone of his dream. Would this thing compel him? Would it carry him with its reflection in his ever more dazzling and dazzled mind across the ancient gap?

A chicken stood on the sidewalk outside the house in which, he knew, Chinese people had recently been living. When he was close to it, the chicken began to move, slowly, into his path, so that he had to stop walking to avoid treading on her. He looked down on the bird, feeling tenderness for her. What kind of life did she have, what could she do? How could she find the crossing? Since childhood he had had the liveliest sympathy for these poor virtually flightless birds, whose life was all scratch and furtiveness and fear and haste, whose life has become a machine, birds who became their own products, eggs, roast fowl, feather pillows. Mostly, he supposed, it was their squalling timidity that touched him, that they would always scatter, looking back nervously at their eternal enemies. To think about it, all creatures were their enemies, men, dogs, cats, other birds, serpents, foxes and weasels, sun and rain. The chicken stood still between his feet.

He looked down on the pepper and salt of her feathers, an uneasy landscape, quivering of the bird herself, or the rustle of parasites in her plumage, or it might be the stirrings of a sea breeze so soft, or not soft at all, but so common that he noticed it not at all on his own hair or skin. Without touching the bird, he could know something about her heat. Close as he was, the chicken did not look up at him, but accepted his legs as part of the natural landscape of terror in which she always lived. They were now a menace, now a refuge. Depending. Things in the world. He did not move. Obscurely, a yearning pity for the creature welled up in him, and more obscurely still, a sad, end-of-the-world feeling that it was this very compassion that all these

years had held him back. For a moment, he played with the plan
of kicking the chicken out of his way. But the opposite of compassion is not cruelty, he understood afresh, not cruelty but
passion. This bird did not hold him back. What held him back
was a fitful wind in him that blew now from sea and now from
shore. He had sought to dignify his soul's delay as Compassion,
when that soul still screamed with hunger for passion. Let him
yearn to be gone—not enough to plan and toil—he had to *want
to be gone.* Let him long to go. He knew he had been there too
long, too long in this coastal district, too long for that matter
standing over the chicken. He had grown comfortable in the
stance of departure. "Good-bye, but never be gone," he quoted to
himself from what source, some poem, his mail, his mind?

The chicken had moved away, back where she had come
from. He looked around, and saw a face, not Chinese, at the
window; was it on guard against any outrage he might have
intended for the chicken, or was it just seeing? He walked on,
beating down the fear that he could never get out because he had
not longed enough to get out, that his life had been all circuit
diagram and no current. Fear must be beaten down, though, he
understood, since fear had nothing to do with the process. With
such consolations, and perhaps a little more, he moved along
towards his conscious room.

For once inside, and the freedom walk over, he gave himself
no liberty to muse or idle. Usually his mood of earnest awareness would start to come over him as he turned onto the prospect and came within a block of his place. Yet perhaps the last
few houses before his, filled with Indians from the interior wordlessly displaced, some of the women still wearing stripes painted
around their muscular legs, thin blue lines at ankle and mid-
shank and just below the knee, he would pass by unperceiving,
while his mind was tuning itself to the superb vacant machine
he would find inside, at the top of the last staircase, his room.
His point of departure. The thirty-two pleasantly creaking
wooden steps were themselves worked into his preparations.
Casual and dreamy he might allow himself to be at the morning
café or while walking home, but this room of his was too deliberate a triumph of his hard work for him to permit himself to

enter with thoughts at random. That he had reached the stairs meant that, for this day once again, the outer way, the way of the street, had failed; mind fixed on the brevity of human life, he had all the more reason to commit himself renewed to the Work of the Room.

Every day at this time when he entered the room, he made the same discovery, and the discovery tended to heal him like the breeze that so often opened from the sea on hot afternoons. To perceive the order he had prepared to leave, this was almost as sweet as leaving. Or as he thought leaving one day would be.

The door of the room had been rehung to swing outward, so he drew it towards him now, walked around it, into the doorhole. To come into the room was part of the process by which he hoped to leave it. With his hands on the doorjambs, it was his business to think about gates and doors, the goings in and comings out. Coming forth. So he would stand, the gates in his hands, hands on the gates, room in his eyes, as if with that simultaneity to open the room itself out past its conventional dimensions. And he would be there, then.

But now, conceding again to the place, putting its nature on, he came into the room. At the edge of the narrow sisal carpet, he toed off his shoes and left them neatly paired. Left foot onto mat, right foot brought beside it. Left foot moves forward, feeling the rough hard knotwork of the mat, right foot follows, to share the weight, the feel. This was the Lame Dance he had copied from Crete and Canaan, thigh-smitten, awry, advancing always by the left. At the far end of the carpet he crouched down on his heels, then sat down cross-legged in one smooth motion, almost gracefully. The one window faced him directly, the eastern sky full of the diffuse brightness of the winter afternoon.

His sitting this way had no reference to Eastern postures. His room had indeed a chair in it, a black sturdy old one from the last century, with a ladder back and finials turned to resemble pineapples. But his orders proposed that chair only for morning and late night, at the window, when he could watch the often indistinguishable place where the sea and marsh came together. He sat like a man whose business it was to sit. Right foot squeezed a little between left thigh and left calf, left foot

relaxed on right thigh, turned out, sole of the foot tenderly exposed, old corn on ball, a long white palm turned up for alms.
Foot very pale in the soft light. Into the female triangle his legs
formed, the male parts of him protruded with a gentle swell
inside the loose trousers. His back curved in a way he would
have been ashamed of years ago, when there was talk of hatha
yoga. His head slumped forward, so his open eyes were looking
now at his hands, also open, also palm up in his lap. That is, they
rested above that female triangle, obscuring it. Little of the female left, he might have thought. Slumped as he was, his mind
widened. He had his own kind of impeccability.

The place he was busy all these years coming from was a
place we all know, or at least have the evidence to know. And he
had been travelling long enough now for a certain sorrow or
ruefulness to have inured in his journey. He smelled it now,
smell of a hand now open that had been closed. Of course as a
child he had rested his hands in the folds and damps of his body
for minutes at a time, later to smell the fragrances they gave off,
as he was coming to know the flower of his body, flower his
body was, to get to know.

The smell now on his hands was transferred from no dewy
original, but was the smell of the hands themselves, hands that
had for years, like all of ours, been kept closed, hands now falling
open. Their own smell.

He saw them, their fingers smudged with newsprint from
the morning papers. In a while, when the time was right, he
would get up in one motion and go into the little bathroom to
wash them. He smiled at the old man in his hands, the one that
wanted to rub the smudgy fingertips clean on his trousers. No,
he answered, no. Wait your time. Then he closed his eyes almost
fully and began his work.

This work of his was a sort of hunting. A man, armed for
the chase, goes out alone in the earliest morning and wanders in
the rocks, clefts and coverts where game might lie hidden. He
walks silently, his mind utterly open to event. He is alert for the
first sign he might be able to read in the endless text of the
world. Not until he finds clear recent spoor will he cease attend-
ing to all other possible textual encounters, and restrict himself

to this one fresh lead. And along he goes, no less silent, but his heart happy with the shift of rhythm, the needs of the doing. Then he finds his beast and slays it.

The landscape in his kind of work was inside, and the beasts were images; he sought them and killed them. No more than that. Always there were failures, limping creatures who crept away maimed but viable still, unharmed things that hurried into the brush, turning back to snarl or flick an insolent scut of tail. But as in most processes where man sets his hand against nature, success far exceeds failure in profitableness. At a clean kill, he'd lift the image up with open eyes and offer it to the nothingness bright beyond the window.

Strange mixed bag of the chase, old remembereds and new desireds, palimpsests of nights, overlay of days, as if he turned a catalogue on soft pulpy paper printed with all the items he'd have to destroy before he could go. Some came back in dream or waking, and then he'd stalk them more deliberately, ignoring likelier game that chanced to happen along, firm in his pursuit of some noumenon that had tricked him before, dead and wouldn't lie down, down and wouldn't die.

He had learned how to take them apart, and that was his weapon. Find them, fix them with an eye, dismantle the sight and the taste and the feel of them, dismantle his own reaction to or from them. Make them go. Gone. His emotions were structures, a house he had been trapped in, and like any other house it could be pulled down, sometimes one board at a time, sometimes a whole wall. He'd been at it for years and the house was still a house, or at least the sturdy ruins of one. And the landscape still teemed with animals. He smiled—he was at least in a hunter's paradise. A sad smile, blank as the sole of his foot. Yet he was winning, he thought, for while the images still abounded, the ecology had changed. Tamer populations moved in, fewer predators, wrathful lions and lecherous panthers mostly gone now, conceptual apes and memorious elephants rare. Mostly now it was bunnies and mice. Little birds.

Every day he would work till an hour before sunset, then rise up quickly and undress to bathe in the tepid water supplied from the old pipes. Naked he would come back into his room

and by the last light pin a large piece of paper to the wall and
swiftly execute the sigil or drawing this day had provided—an
unplanned, sudden releasement into space of what the interior
had taught him. It was the emblem of each day, and his only
visible archive of it. His hands would work quickly, often while
his eyes were closed. The finished sheet would be examined
once, in the window, and then be settled face-down on a thick
pile of earlier drawings, a heap of signs stacked neatly on a low
table in the corner of the room. He would not look at these
again. Now he was free to stand at the window again, a little
away from it, and with his eyes fixed on the darkening sky,
carefully dismantle in his mind the sign or image he had just
drawn.

That left him free to dress, ever in white at this hour, and
leave the room. The last part of daytime, before his walk to the
café, involved what was by far the most frontal of all his ap-
proaches to his problem. He had spent years in friendship with
the sun, and always had a good sense of where the sun was in the
sky, even on a day like today when it had not once appeared in
its proper person. He thought of it now, of *her*, since he understood the sun that way, and set his back to her as soon as he had
come down onto the street. Behind him, straight behind him,
she would be setting now. He walked away, thus due east, guid-
ing himself always by that sense of her behind him; toward
marsh and sea he moved, stepping briskly on the squelchy
ground, hopping the little tidal puddles, making for the beach
itself. When he got there, he'd kick his sandals off and start to
run hard down the darkish compacted sand until he came to the
actual surf. Here he'd stand, the water around his ankles sloshing in and out, scooping out the sand from beneath his feet so
that every few waves he'd have to lift a foot and let the sand
resettle smooth beneath it. This vigil continued till she had fully
set behind him and even the trailing shimmer of her personality
would be gone, he knew, from the western sky, and the sky in
front of him was completely black. This was the end of his time.
The time between day and night, land and sea, had always been
his, his to haunt him, never his to hold. Tonight as he turned
back, he began to suspect that this between-time was not a

knowing and not a knowledge, but might be only one more image, just another one to be undone, a romantic fetch sent from his youth to trick him in his age. He made up his mind to hunt it down the next day.

Now he could turn from the sea and find his way back to the places where people lived. Dinnertime. As he stepped, less nimbly now, over the marshy earth clotted with grasses, he kept his eyes on the ground. Under the first street-light, he noticed that his white shirt was spotted all over with wet spots from the ocean spray; the wet dark pattern reminded him of the pepper-and-salt chicken he had looked down at in the afternoon. Or perhaps the stance of walking slowly while looking down brought the bird to mind. Tears came into his eyes for the futility of this life around him, of his own life, futile too, but somehow not as futile as those others' were, since he, with what chance of success? at least was striving to be gone. By the next street lamp, two hundred feet up the road, he saw that his shirt was already drying in the land breeze that came to meet him.

The Book and Its Contents

I find it difficult to tell what little of the truth I may know, now that Dr. Perkunas is dead. Nature and experience have combined to make me a close-mouthed, unforthcoming, scant forgiving sort of man, and seldom do I feel the need to proffer what I think I know, little as it is. People have enough to do avoiding their own truths.

Still, I was his patient, and, as small towns measure these things, his friend. I knew him not as well as I know myself, but disliked him less, so I can bear the town's characterization. Towns know nothing of real friendship, ardent symposiums of those whose rhythms of perception and permission are meaningful together. But the town knows me, after all. I was born here, as my father was, and though I've spent most of my life away, those years aren't real time for a town. A town counts only the overall contact, and presumes to understand what one of its own is up to no matter how far he goes or how long he stays. He's away (painting in Paris, whoring in Managua, praying in Wandrille) and then he's back, and the "away" is just an idiosyncrasy, like a taste for pink shirts or a fondness for old expletives like "judaspriest!"

Dr. Perkunas had settled in the town, taking over old Jarvis's practice, just about the time I made my way home from five years in Asia. I came to see him about some skin thing I'd picked up in Nepal, and didn't expect him to be much help. Nor was he, but he did give me the obvious antibiotics that probably kept whatever it was from getting worse. It healed eventually, as bodies do, and I came back to get a Nunc dimittis from him.

This time I noticed a fastidious nervousness in the man. For a moment he left the office to get some cigarettes—he was a heavy smoker—and I could see through the door into his private apartments a number of bookcases congested with what clearly were not medical books. I alluded to these on his return, readers are rare in my town, and he seemed torn between discussion and discretion, as I might once have been before the latter triumphed once for all in what passes for my character. The other triumphed now in him, and he began, as if both weary and excited at once, to talk about his researches into language.

I made civil enough queries, and came up with some linguistic oddities from my travels, but he received these only impatiently, as if by language he did not mean something people did, speaking well or ill or interestingly; he seemed to mean by language something vast and principled, of which any practical application (communication, expression, history)) was a tiresome irrelevance, an unfortunate lapse of the Absolute into mere behavior.

He talked on, and when his consultation hours drew to a close, led me into his sitting room and went on talking. He gave me supermarket teabag tea and Social Tea biscuits; as long as I knew him, I never saw him serve, or eat, anything else.

His talk as such did not interest me much, but it was pleasing to hear a fellow human speak with passion about a subject that had nothing to do with the town, the nation, or public affairs of the great or small. We might just as well have been in Copenhagen, and I felt enlarged by the liberality of his abstruseness. Indeed the only local reference I ever heard him make was to the name of our state, which he pronounced strangely, each of its five syllables stated with equal emphasis, though all the rest of us pronounce it with four, heavy stress on the third. The name fascinated him, as names in general did—not to be sure as a heraldry of character or personality of the bearers, but as a sort of topological mapping of a prime reality. The actual miles and mills of Pennsylvania were just premature reification, a rash materialization of what should truly have stayed latent in a pure potency the name both signified and, somehow, *was*.

He was balding, grizzled, brownish, with ear tufts. His grey eyes were too light for his dusky skin, and his skin too tight for his bones. He never looked comfortable. I hope he sometimes was, though. A world without comfort is not worth pursuing. Maybe he was at ease in that four-hour stretch—six to ten—he gave himself every morning for reading.

What did he read? Patterns. Strings. Never books. Books were just zoos where you went to look at paragraphs. He had many books, but never added to their number. Even with my perfunctory education I could see he was scarcely literate in any cultural tradition, and remarkably ill-informed. But like a medieval monk, he contemplated with enthusiasm what he did not find it necessary to understand.

Our relationship, meagerly established, neither grew nor declined, but proved to have the austere durability of desert plants. Once a week I would stop in after his evening hours and listen to him rave. It was like those weary friendships that arise from a shared interest, say in chess, and never care, or dare, to transcend the occasion of their genesis. But with Dr. Perkunas, I was not even put to the inconvenience of playing a game, or bothering myself with attacks, gambits, endgames. Enough to listen. With him, we were always in the middle of things; nothing ever started, and nothing ever ended.

Once I took the liberty of bringing him, all neatly typed out, a passage that had struck me in an old notebook of my own I was rereading. Evidently I had copied it out without bothering to identify the source—an omission that would not trouble Perkunas. I handed him the crisp paper, and he read it aloud to me, his East European singsong sounding very peculiar chanting the very English passage:

> *What it says, sire, is less than it means. That is the trick of words, and their troth too, to which they are ever faithful, as a shadow to its man. . . . There is a sunlight too of words, and days overcast, and simple night. But the word rides through, and what it means takes flesh in the new day, or as the day, and the word walks around in the plain morning, exploring the dewy grass of the garden of what it means.*

He laid the paper on top of the plate of biscuits, and looked at me. There was something of fear in his eyes, and a surmise about me I had never seen before in him. He took his glasses off and rubbed their lenses on his trouser leg, put them on his nose again and picked up the paper once more. Silently this time he studied it; he seemed to read it straight through three or four times. He laid it on the table now, beside the plate, so the cookies were available again—perhaps he had convinced himself of my good intentions. Or, more likely, considering what was to come, of my ignorance.

"The word walks around," he quoted. And looked at me. I confess to a shiver that wriggled up my spine at that moment as I guessed what startling literalness—half crucifixion and half cartoon—that phrase might have for his naive sensibilities. He thanked me, nonetheless, for bringing him the citation (he called it that), and then made signs that told me our evening had come to a close. I left with less than the usual sense of boredom and inconsequentiality that typically haunted my walk home from our weekly discussions. As I passed under the great larches by the cemetery, golden now for October, I even detected in myself a certain excitement, as if there were more to Perkunas's obsessions than a complex crossword puzzle. I nibbled my Social Tea Biscuit slowly, and it lasted me half the way home.

Yet next week was like old times, and the week after, and the week after that. Things were pleasant and comfortable, and Perkunas talked, and I listened and nibbled and sipped and listened. All the rest of the week, as the town could tell you, I am a formidable talker, so this evening with Perkunas, I must admit, had its charm for me, a turnabout, a releasement. The usual current of our verbal lassitude idled along.

Then one week in early December Perkunas, instead of having a stack of books precarious on the arm of his stuffed chair, had only a sheaf of papers on his lap. He made no reference to these for an hour or so, then, after one of his infrequent pauses, he had lifted the papers to his eyes (blocking my view of his face), looked through them slowly, lowered them and looked at me in a way I could only find challenging.

"And doubted every door forever more," he said.

"I beg your pardon?"

He repeated the sentence. In my drowsiness, I had not only missed the words, but was slow at gathering that he was quoting, not remarking. I pulled myself together and asked what it was from. It doesn't matter, he said, and repeated the sentence yet again, and began to talk.

My own state led me to think about the proposition the words made, and thus I lost the drift of his remarks. In truth I was sleepy, with that after-dinner winter sleepiness that I would take as a sign of advancing age if I had not felt it all my life—though even as a child it made me feel like an old man. Perhaps we are all ages at all times, and can be ourselves as we will be in fifty years right now, by an effort. Or is it by a release of effort? By the time I could get my mind back onto what Dr. Perkunas was saying, he was on terrain familiar to me from this monomaniac's conversation.

"Every door is every one. No exceptions. And doubt is absolute. No paradox. To doubt everything is doubt nothing, isn't it. True. *Dubio*, to be uncertain, to raise difficulties about. The absolute insists again, no?, in forevermore, one word. Always and everything. But a thing here is a door. Nothing else is mentioned as being doubted. What are the words telling us?"

That's how he talked. Now he paused on that ritual self-invitation to expatiate that his last words comprised. Politely, as usual, he waited a civil ten seconds to see if I'd offer an answer to what, after all, he may have not meant only as a rhetorical question. Maybe he really wanted to know, maybe even more desperately wanted someone to tell him what the words are ever telling us. Maybe he wanted a woman's soft voice to whisper the answer on his real pillow. But there were no women in his life, as far as I could tell. He went on:

"To doubt a door is doubting in and out, both. Stasis. The old greek Flux, panta rhei, the pratityasamutpada of the Buddhist people, the interdependency ever-crossing never-ending—all of that, here negated. This is a Jewish Christian despair, my friend, be sure of it. No pagan ever doubted a door. But see now where it leaves us, this doubted door. Bleak, bleak, bleak. Nothing else is mentioned, so everything else is possible. Only the door, only the door."

"Excuse me," I said, "I don't feel the weight of despondency you do in the phrase. Maybe the context instructs you to read the words so pessimistically. They are sad, surely, and a bit overemphatic with that lugubrious "nevermore"; but it's just a sentence, limited. What does it mean in the whole context? And what is the sentence from, by the way?"

"Context has nothing to do with it!" He came close to shouting. "Context is gossip. Context is just sociology, the conspiracy of triviality in which language is enmeshed in this bad world. We don't need a context—we have words!"

He paused on that exaltation, then subsided. After a few moments, he half-apologetically (for the outburst? for the fact he was about to acknowledge?) admitted that the phrase was his own, from a poem he'd written in medical school. He had been in love, and once, visiting his girl friend, had (by divine inspiration, he said) paused at her door before knocking on it. He heard a male voice uttering tendresses within, and he crept away and never spoke to the girl again. But that's not the point, he assured me. It's not why the words got written, but what they say. What do they *say?* he crowed, as if the question were an all-vanquishing rebuttal.

I did want to hear about his romance, but I accepted, by my silence, the return of the conversation to our usual matters, which languidly engaged us for the rest of the evening.

That year I spent the Christmas season with my parents in Florida, where they'd moved twenty years ago. They had a little place on the west coast, half of a bitty island, and I bloated and swam and bamboozled some local ladies, then came back north to spend the weekend of New Year's with a dear friend in Massachusetts. So it wasn't till the second week in January that I visited Perkunas again; I had a bad cold to bring him, which he brusquely dealt with before we settled down to chat.

The first surprise was Perkunas himself; he looked worn and aged, and his skin, even allowing for my recent sojourn among the goldentanned, seemed really grey, ashen. And above the doorway leading to an inner room was hanging a big spray of mistletoe. I had never known Perkunas to observe any custom, religious or secular, and cocked an eyebrow at it with a smile. He waved at it vaguely and said they did that in his country and why not. Why not indeed, I agreed, and the subject lapsed. I reverted to my first surprise, and asked him about his health. He just shook his head, took off his glasses, put them on, shook his head again and looked at me, as if to examine my comprehension of these signs. Were they the acted-out symptoms of some ailment? I looked back at him and waited, expecting either a verbal answer, or a shift to our usual topics. Instead, he closed his eyes and laid his head against the back of his old kroehler.

Why not follow his example, I thought, and did so. My chair was just as comfortable, if newer, and I let my mind range whatever it found in the way of recent imagery while I waited for Perkunas to have something to say. I had been doing not much of anything for several weeks, and there is nothing more exhausting than inactivity, especially a pleasant inactivity with family and girlfriend and snow and eating and drinking and watching television with people you know too well to bother talking with. I drifted, but was not asleep. I certainly was not asleep.

"Come, I have to show you something." When I opened my eyes I found Perkunas on his feet, inclined a little toward me as if caught in mid-bow. I rose and followed him to the doorway hung with mistletoe.

I don't have much more to tell, and I'm conscious of a desire to stretch things out, record unnecessary details (the pale green paint on the door woodwork, the smell of cherries, the pulled thread on Perkunas' dark red necktie) to flesh out the hurried conclusion of my story. I said at the beginning that I knew little of the truth, and I wasn't lying. All I can give any account of is this last passage, upcoming, in my relationship with Dr. Perkunas. Now that I know it was the last, it takes on peculiar emphases and shadings. But even at the time it felt like a curious and important moment. I had never been in any other room of his private apartment, and the prospect of entering one now excused, if it did not explain, the odd feeling of excitement that came over me. Yes, mixed with a little fear. But then I am often afraid, truth to tell, and fear is such a common music we hardly need admit to hearing it.

And I am stretching, too, because I have been so long-winded in bringing us to this moment, to a crisis about which I can offer only some inferences, if that. Maybe just by talking more and more I can make the end of my account balance its beginnings—a deathbed fancy; I'm sure the dying man begs for the energy and opportunity to make the whole argosy into the underworld take as long as his life's whole progress to that moment of departure. Enough of this procrastination—open the door.

Dr. Perkunas opened the door and, ever polite, stood aside so I might enter first. The room I entered was bare except for a wooden table not quite at the center, a lightbulb hanging above it, a wooden chair at an angle in front of it, its back to one entering the room. On the table was a book, which even at this distance was obviously hand-bound, a big thick quarto. If there was a window in the room, it was hidden behind a long drape off to the side.

"Go up to it, look at it. It is what I do. Or what I have done, done with it all. It is almost finished now, after so long. Go look. You can touch it, even. Look." Dr. Perkunas was speaking in a calm, even tender voice.

There seemed no harm in humoring him. The book, close up, was buckram, a little rumpled with the glue that held it to the boards, and the three-quarter leatherette binding was irregular. But the whole book was sound, solid to the feel. I opened it at random and found the heavy pages inscribed closely, in a neat, tiny, quite legible handwriting. At first I thought it was pencil, then saw it was a curious pale grey ink. I thumbed through the pages and saw no divisions, no chapter beginnings, large letters, blank spaces. It was one continuity of text. I turned back to the first page—no title, no mark of commencement. On the flyleaf was written Perkunas' full name, then the text began on the first recto page and went on. The last eight leaves of the book were still blank. I estimate four to five hundred pages were in the book, all densely written. At random I chose a passage in the middle and began to read:

> . . . *manner in which this act is performed—its degree of intensity and the rituals employed—appears on the*

contrary that the octahedral form is seldom seen in
India, with the circles changed into squares. They
seem to have been successful at first, then the perfect
light will pour out upon everyone. This is an appro-
priate point to remind the reader that in Guiana the
rainbow is called by the name of the opossum. This is
the excellent foppery of the world . . .

I looked up at Perkunas and let the book close. I cannot vouch
for the exact wording, but what I set down here is the drift of
what I read. And drift is what it seemed to be.

"What is this, Doctor?"

"It is my book, the book. It is a book the words have written
by themselves." He smiled at me as he said this, a shy smile,
modest, betokening an artist's humility not even his obvious
metabolic excitement could confute. "It is a book where only
language exists, and language tells. It says everything by itself,
without our intrusion and our interferences. I have guided its
grammar—people are so fussy about grammar, as if language
couldn't be trusted . . ." What had begun as a pleasantry seemed
to trail off. He looked nervously behind him at the open doorway, where the mistletoe jiggled a little in a draft from somewhere.

I tried to draw him back to the book. "I don't understand
the passage I just read. Do I have to read it from the beginning?"

"Of course not. There is no beginning. You would understand if you read slowly, and thought about every word as it
came along. And they do. They do."

He sat down on the chair. Unlike him to leave the guest
standing—but his next words explained.

"Go out. Go out into the next room and watch, look at me
here, at the desk. But don't come in until I tell you to. Go."

His voice was urgent now, and there was no sense of an
intellectual argument energetically pursued. It seemed urgent
the way real things in the world can be, dangerous, fleeable. I
went into the familiar sitting room and stood at the door looking
in at him.

He took the book from the table where I'd laid it, and,

opening it at random, began to read in a quiet voice. I could not hear the words.

But in a few minutes I began to see them. That's how it felt, at any rate. Certainly I began to see. A peacock came first, and walked unconcernedly across the room, through the doctor's legs, and vanished in the spray of a fountain that appeared just in time to receive the bird, then itself disappeared just in the spot where three women were coming toward me till a ship in sail obscured them as it passed, making great waves, into a forest in which it could still be seen. An elephant followed the path of the peacock, and a small sports coupe from the 1920s followed the elephant. At its wheel a goggled man cried out in pain as a rainstorm soaked the white linen of his duster. A small city grew in the distance between the doctor's shoulder blades, and was wiped out by fire while two dozen schoolgirls in straw hats and grey uniforms scampered by holding baskets of flowers—lupines and phlox. All these things were transparent, in the sense that through them I could see table and doctor and book and far wall, yet they had the quality of being realer than their ground. And the wall and the doctor and so on were transparent too, and through them I could see continuous motion, both in the evident space of the room, and in more paradoxical planes within them or athwart them. There was a rich and intricate blur of movement and stillness, yet at any given moment one being or one thing clearly was the focal point of this local reality—no doubt the word leaving the doctor's mouth at that same moment.

Then another order of presence made itself known. A tall figure, dark in form, seemed to take on a different kind of transparency, and lingered in that steady state while all the other words, things, signs, whatever they were, focused and gradually blurred away. This form, perhaps a man's, now began to move toward me, or toward the doorway. I could see no face beneath the cowl it wore, only a pullulation of tiny images, as if that face too were a plane of event on which unscrupulous multitudes of words came and went. The curious thing approached the door, and I was uneasy enough to shrink away. I assured myself the apparition was just that, an illusion. *But what isn't?*, a nasty voice demanded inside my head. And some illusions are more energetic than others, fearful, with staying power. This thing with the leprous face mottled with unknown actions done by unknown actors in some other world came to the doorway, but did not cross the threshold. It looked at me and I endured its examination—there was no singleness about the thing, and being watched by it felt like being observed by a pack of dogs or a cage of monkeys. This was oddly comforting to me, along with an unarguable certainty that the mistletoe hung up kept it from coming into this room. Without turning at all, it moved away, moved back—or at least grew smaller so our usual sense of perspective said, it is going away. Its intensity of horror—was it that, or was it just an intensity of complexity itself that so rippled from it?—did not diminish with size. I reached forward and pulled the door closed.

The book, when I had looked at it a while ago, had felt unpleasant, as if the futility I felt inspired it had reached a level of intensity for which the emotions which composed it were not intended—trivial tragedy, paroxysmal vapidity. It had a late night feeling, smelled of empty chatter by people too tired to make sense, too lonely to go home—you know the feeling, diners have it at three A.M., and church suppers at eight P.M. The way we clutch to each other for what, for precisely what, we cannot give—that was the taste of that book.

How harsh my judgment was! How unfair to my old friend! Here I was leaving him alone in that weird room with whatever it is. For all I knew, I was projecting my own dominant mood onto that book, for was I not prime example of just such a wearied, lonely, clutching man? I could be braver. I tapped on the door with my fingertips and called out my friend's name. No response. I knocked again, with knuckles this time, and silence again. I had enough integrity to turn the knob and try to go in. To my great relief, the door had locked itself when I closed it. "Perkunas!" I cried, "I have to be getting home now. Call me tomorrow, will you? Good night!" I was trying to talk as if everything were the same as everything else, no difference, no problem. I waited a few moments, said good night again, and left his apartment. I did not, of course, ever see my friend again.

As I walked along the idle streets, empty at the best of times in our dull town, I felt a predictable yearning for crowds, for companionship of the most unimaginative type. Though I rate myself a coward, I overcame that impulse and contented myself with the fierce cold air, dry, the stars' blaze overhead, Orion in particular, balanced on Rigel, gave an air of firm settledness to the visible world I found bracing. Less out of fear (was the thing following me? how would I deal with the doctor hereafter, after this unprecedented but vastly embarrassing revelation of his real concerns?) than out of a wish to get the book and its contents out of my head, I took the faintheart course of spending the night at a dear friend's house. She made me coffee and gave me cookies, and didn't examine too closely my motives for wanting to sleep with her.

By nine the next morning, when she and I were up and about, having brunch at the Swan, the whole thing, as you probably remember, was over. Later that week, our town paper (the *Democrat*, though we haven't elected one since the Civil War) gave as full an account of the puzzling incident as we're ever likely to read.

A car full of workers on their way to a construction site saw the doctor, fully clothed but without an overcoat, running down the middle of the street in the frozen dawn light. They saw him dart into the park near the bandstand; they noted in particular that he leaped the big pile of snow at roadside without breaking stride. One of the workers had frequently, and successfully, consulted the doctor about his bad back; at his request, the other workers stopped the car and came into the park to make sure the doctor was all right. When they got there, they couldn't be sure if he was or not. They saw the man standing in front of the bandstand, where in summer a circle of grass invited recliners. As they watched, he opened two or three buttons of his shirt and reached in with both hands. One of the watchers compared the doctor's movements at that point to those of a friend of his who used to walk around keeping his pet ferrets in his shirt—quick, anxious a little, but in control. None of the men thought he looked afraid. But they were frightened when they saw him begin to pull out of his clothes and scatter on the snow in front of him, one after another, a bunch of bananas, a roller skate, a lighted candle, a football, a cat, a steam iron, a chessboard with men on it, handfuls of what looked like money, a glass of water that steamed in the cold air and sat upright in the snow when he let it fall. All the objects lay about, except the cat, which scampered away and was seen no more.

The workers, alerted perhaps by the money, began to move closer to the doctor, and the pace of his productions increased. Now a blinding confusion of objects and animals began to be pulled out and strewn, so many in fact that they began to float rather than fall, float across the snow until they found a place to settle. The workers saw not just things and creatures coming out, but even what they described as "moods"—sheets of pure color that shimmered substantially before dissolving, huge shapes "made out of sound."

About this time they began to hear the doctor's voice, or at least some voice that synchronized with the movements of Perkunas's lips, though the sound seemed to come from up above, a huge voice, but of a man speaking very gently, the workers said, for all its volume, "loud, but not shouting, just talking quietly but very, very loud" is how one of them described it. The voice was so powerful that they stopped moving, and the air was thick with things the doctor was pulling out of himself and throwing into the world. As they watched, he began to rise into the air, they all swear to this, and when he was high enough for them to see the ridgepole of the bandstand roof just under his heels, the torrent of creations swept down on them and they were lost in sheer thingliness.

By the time they had dug themselves out, strangely unhurt by the sensed weight of all the things that had floated, not fallen, down on them, they could not see the doctor anywhere. Around the place he'd been standing were only his tracks in the snow, going in, standing. And then he went up.

That was the story they told, and absurd as it sounded, no one had any more convincing way of accounting for the disappearance of Dr. Perkunas, and of the presence in the park of so many thousands of unlikely, even preposterous, items. By full daylight the police and fire volunteers had been joined by most of the idle townspeople, all of them busy carrying off whatever they could get their hands on. By the time my friend and I had heard the story by word of mouth and gotten over to the park, most of the treasures, if that's what they were, were gone. Monica helped herself to a little French prayerbook, *Le Paroissien mystique,* and I took away with me a single roller skate. It has no maker's mark on it. I keep it over my fireplace, and sit in front of it from time to time, wondering what really happened, to the town and to Perkunas. Nothing made any sense to me. It was a pity that the workers had no intellectual preparation for being witnesses of what they beheld; people of theological cultivation might have understood things quite differently. As it was, we had a marvel, but no material for thinking about it with. Confronted with the inexplicable, the mind has a comforting slovenly habit of going back, or forward, to countryside it thinks it can negotiate. I too stopped thinking about it after a while. And the town had, as towns do, other things on its mind.

A few days later I went back and sat in Perkunas's apartment. The door to that room stood open, and the book, the wicked or peculiar or wonderful book, sat on the table. The apartment was just as it had been, and there was some talk of a cousin from Gettysburg coming up the next weekend and settling his affairs. I decided to take the book away with me, and not leave it as a trap for someone even less prepared than I to cope with its powers.

In the following weeks I mourned my old friend placidly from time to time. Soon it was clear that the book shouldn't stay with me. So I sent it along, together with a more circumstantial account of it and him than I give here, to the Fortean Museum in Philadelphia, a small place open one afternoon a week to the general public. You will find the book there, with my fuller statement, in the gallery that examines Manifestation. They cross-index it in their catalogue also under the listing Conjurations and Spells, Bad Effects of. This category is clearly nonsense, unless we choose to regard the whole panoply of human language as one interminable magic spell that long, long ago got utterly out of control.

The Hole

Sonia T, a tall attractive blonde woman in her late twenties, was ironing clothes. It was four o'clock in the afternoon on a day in late October, very bright and rather warm. Earlier she had walked in the park and done a little shopping. She had no plans for making dinner; she hoped that when her husband, Edward, came home, she could induce him to go out for dinner, something they did once or twice a week. They had been married for three years, and she was happy, and told her friends so, and they had no reason to suspect she was dissembling. In a year or so, she planned to have Edward's child; its names were already a topic for pillow-talk.

She had ironed several of his shirts, though the stay-pressed cotton didn't really need it, along with several blouses of her own that did, silks and Indian ramies, for example, and a pretty, loose-fitting cotton shawl-collared tunic from Ecuador she liked very much. She ran the iron over a few pairs of white jeans casually, since she was about to put them away for the winter.

Her walk in the park, it may have been, or the lively bustle of today's shopping mall, had excited her a little, and she felt a restless pressure way below her navel, where her thighs gently squeezed in time with the sweeps of her arm sliding the iron along. She was eager for Edward to get home; they could make love quickly, then go for a nice meal. She brought her attention back to the ironing board. Really, there were only a few more garments to go. Then she'd have a bath, get dressed, and wait for Edward.

Next in line was a short straight skirt of heavy white cotton, one that looked good with almost any top, and suited her long legs and trim hips. She tended to wear it well into autumn, and now planned to wear it once more on the next bright warm day that came along. She spread it out on the soft padding of the ironing board, and flicked a few fingertips of water on it from a pudding dish that stood at the square end of the board—just as she had seen her mother do since her earliest days. She knew that steam irons didn't really need such procedures, but she liked the feel of the water and the flick of the fingers, the little speckles of damp that patterned the cloth. She began pressing the skirt with long smooth even strong strokes that each time brought her loins against the edge of the ironing board.

She pulled the skirt around to work on the back. Again she flicked water on the fabric, and watched with pleasure the little plumes of steam rise as the hot iron passed over the wet spots, leaving a smooth crisp wake. Experimentally, she splattered a good deal more water for the next pass, and let the iron stand a moment on the wettest spot, and liked watching the steam gush up around the curved nose of the iron, and the clean hot smell and slightly crushed hot look of the cloth when she lifted the iron. Even more water next time, and she left the iron longer too, even pressing down a little, firmly, then lifting quickly. She wondered how long she dared leave the iron without singeing the cloth.

The center of the skirt she positively soaked, and the iron hissed loudly as it kissed the cloth. She pressed up against the ironing board and counted to six, then seven, then decided to make it ten. At eleven she lifted the iron slowly, and found a faint but definite scorch mark, outline of the iron's prow, left on the cloth. It would never come out. She was angry at herself, and felt stupid for damaging her lovely skirt, but even so she felt a thrill of fulfilment. Her breath came shallow. Carefully she fitted the iron back into the outline mark it had made, and pressed down as hard as she could, and kept it there.

–2–

It wasn't till next morning that Edward finally couldn't keep himself from getting in touch with the police. He had spent a miserable night, prey to anxiety and fantasies and dread, hardly sleeping.

He had examined his conscience in every particular he could reach, and found nothing to reproach himself for in his conduct of their relationship. He went over and over all the details of their engagement and marriage, and every item he could piece together of their history over the last few days. He came to the conclusion that there was no reason for Sonia to leave him of her own free will, no sudden visitors who would scoop her up and carry her out of time. Therefore she had not left under her own free will, so the police were in order. None of her friends and relatives had seen her or heard from her. What else could he do?

After waiting only two or three minutes in the comfortable lounge of the suburban police station, Edward was able to tell his story, meager as it was, to the officer on duty, who promised to do all he could to locate Mrs T, or at least to discover what had become of her. Although, as he pointed out reasonably enough, the story Mr T had given the police was very little to go on. This is, in substance, what Edward had told the police:

Edward had reached his apartment at 6:05 exactly, the usual time, after an uneventful bus trip from midtown Manhattan and a short drive through commuter traffic from the bus station. He had put his car in the underground garage, noting that his wife's Toyota was in its adjacent slot, its hood quite cool—he admitted with a blush that he often felt the hood to see how long before him she'd gotten home.

In the apartment, everything was in order. He had observed with a slight sense of disappointment that nothing had been prepared for dinner, but he enjoyed eating out, and thought they'd go to the new Szechuan restaurant that he'd read about in the next town west. Everything was as it should be, at first glance, except that his wife was not there. He imagined she was visiting with some friend, of whom she had half a dozen in the large condo complex, or perhaps was working out on the Nautilus in the basement spa and had lost track of the time. Edward made himself a cup of instant Sanka and took a plate of chocolate chip cookies into the living room, and watched the local

news. When he stood up during a commercial to go to the bathroom he noticed in the foyer between dressing room and bathroom a neat pile of ironed clothes, with the ironing board still
standing erect.

Only then did he notice that the white skirt on the ironing
board had a deep black burn in it. The iron itself was still plugged in, but turned off by its own controls, and cool to the touch.
The burn in the skirt when he examined it proved to go right
through the fabric, both thicknesses of it, right down into the
ironing board pad and cover itself, right down to the bare wood
now scorched a uniform dull black. He stared at it, baffled, then
went back to the t.v. A certain uneasiness began to steal over
him now, which he tried to calm by imaging a likely scenario:
inattentive, Sonia had let the iron burn a big hole in her favorite
skirt. Distressed, she had gone out for a walk, to shake off the
disappointment and bad mood. He resolved to buy her another
skirt just like it. He knew the clothes she liked, he paid attention to such things, he liked her clothes. He too felt a little
nostalgia for the burnt skirt.

–3–

In the days to come, Edward said nothing at work about his
bereavement. Despite the efforts of the police, nothing was
learned of Sonia's whereabouts. She had been seen in the park in
mid-afternoon, neighbors had met her shopping in the mall, the
woman down the hall had seen her coming up the elevator at
three-thirty, had seen her go into the apartment and close the
door behind her. Nothing more. Despite Edward's wait before
telling the police, or because of it, perhaps, no suspicion at-
tached to him. He had been seen at the usual times and places.
The police visited and examined everything, paying a lot of attention to the ironing board, the only unusual item in it. A
laboratory confirmed the obvious visual impression: the hole
had been burned by the iron.

As the days passed, Edward's anxiety grew deeper, and like
many deep things, ceased to show on the surface. Eventually he
himself began to forget the anxiety, or to think he was forgetting

it. Every now and again he would just think of Sonia as if she
were still there. For several weeks, he did not even make any
effort to see other women, even though it seemed likely enough
to him that he would not soon see Sonia again.

Then one day Edward found a letter in the mailbox when he
came home from work, an odd, crumpled ungainly envelope
ill-stuffed with paper. His address was typed, and the envelope
looked as if it had suffered around the world on its way to him.
Edward read all his other mail, even the bills and flyers, before
he let himself sit down at the kitchen table to look at this
peculiar message. To begin with, the stamps were foreign, of
course. After a while, he made out with the help of pictures of
palm trees and whitish ruins that the letter had been mailed in
the Republic of Cyprus, a nation that he connected vaguely with
Greece and Israel and Turkey, and with war. Halfway between
them? The envelope was blue and flimsy, and had no return
address. He tore it open carefully, to save the stamp for the
bookkeeper's little boy.

Inside, he was shocked to find a letter from his wife, in her
own hand, her typical bold, vague penmanship. This is what it
said:

> *Dear Edward,*
>
> *I am in hell, and I'm glad. It is a strange place,
> and I'm happy, and it's strange that I'm happy but I
> am, I'm not sure if I'll ever be able to come back or if I
> even want to—though you know I really do love you.
> It's funny, I love you and I miss you, sometimes I
> miss you a lot, but I don't want to come back. Why is
> that? Maybe you can figure it out, sometimes you
> know these things, sometimes you know me better
> than I know myself. I really love you, honey. It must
> be terrible for you to be alone, I'm sorry I left the way
> I did. But I didn't know I was leaving, even, till I was
> already gone, and then it was too late to come back or
> even leave you a letter. I don't want you to be lonely, I
> don't mind if you find another woman, but be careful,
> look around and take your time, don't get caught too*

*quickly. See a lot of girls and see what happens. It
seems dumb for me to be giving you advice, I'm sorry,
baby, I still feel we're together, even after what I did.*

*I was ironing and I could hardly wait for you to
get home. I got distracted at one point and scorched
my white skirt, and I got mad when I saw I ruined it,
so I shoved the iron down and made a real burn. It
was stupid, I guess, but I really was mad, and wanted
to break something so I just burned the skirt. Like
breaking a plate. Then I was afraid it would start a
fire, so I pulled the iron up and turned it off. The burn
went right through the skirt and actually burned the
iron-board. I looked at the black burn mark and it
was still smoking, and somehow I couldn't stop looking at it.*

*The longer I looked at it, the bigger it seemed to
be, until eventually it looked like a big hole, a big
black hole that went down and down, all the way to
the middle of the earth. I don't know how I did it, or
how it happened, but I started to climb into the hole,
and walked down it like a long tunnel that slopes. I
mean it was walking, not falling. And I kept walking.
Once I turned around and I saw the light behind me,
our apartment, but it didn't look like that, it looked
like trees and sky up there, so I kept going down. It
was dark but it wasn't scary or like night, just dark
and soft and warm. I could even see the time on my
wristwatch: it was 4:15, and I figured I'd still have
plenty of time to get back before you got home. After
a while the tunnel ended and things got bigger. I was
in a huge place like a park, and there was a castle in
the distance, and dark trees, some kind of pines, and
a lot of people moving around. I wasn't frightened of
them at all, I don't know why. It was warmer here,
and I decided to take my clothes off, and I did. I just
let them fall on the grass. I liked feeling the way I felt,
and I walked toward the castle. Then some people
came along and they were naked too, and didn't say*

*anything, just took me gently by both arms and led
me along to the castle gate. When we got inside, all
the rooms were pretty empty, and they left me in one
of them. I looked out the window and there were
children playing down on the lawn, rolling a ball from
one to another, silvery, the only bright thing I saw
down there. One of them looked up at me and he had
the face of an old man. So I went away from the
window and stood in the middle of the room. I stood
very straight.*

*Then a man came in. This is the part you won't
like, I'm sorry, but I'm not ashamed. You can call me
a slut if it makes you feel better but it's not like that.
He came in, he wasn't young exactly, but not old
either. He didn't say anything, but I knew he was the
king or whatever of this place. He just came over to
me and began to kiss me. I liked it, a lot. Then he lay
me down on the ground, and it wasn't the floor any
more but a soft black grass that smelled like cloves
and onions and roses all together. He made love to me
and I let him, and I had an orgasm that lasted a long
time. Maybe it's still going on.*

*He is the king and he doesn't have a name, and
he doesn't call me any name, but he treats me like his
wife. Once I tried to tell him that I was already married, and that I loved my husband. He wasn't upset,
and didn't seem to get jealous, he just said that you
were up there and I was down here, and that was all
that counted.*

*He says this place is where the dead go, when
people die who haven't done anything special in their
lives, and that you up there would call the place hell.
But there's no suffering here, and people make love
and have a good time. But it's pretty quiet, since
there's no music. At least I haven't heard any, and
once I tried to whistle and it sounded stupid in this
castle. Nobody stopped me, though. I have a wonderful big room, and there are servants who take care of
me, and bring me anything I want.*

One day I asked him why he chose me for his wife. He said he had other wives but he really had chosen me. He said he found me beautiful and that I had a lot of energy in sex (as you know), but that I was also very brave, and had done a brave thing. I didn't understand that, but he wouldn't explain. Unless he means climbing down the hole, but that seems just curiosity to me.

Anyhow, when I ask him about going back to you he gets vague, and says you probably wouldn't want me any more. I have no right to ask you if that's true, so I won't. But I want to tell you the truth—I am happy here, and don't think I really do want to go back, though it would be nice to know that I could if I wanted to.

I pestered him about how worried you must be, so he suggested I send you a letter. I don't know why I didn't think of it, but anyhow here it is, your guilty wife's explanation. I hope you'll forgive me and still love me somehow, no matter what you do. It's good to know that somebody loves you. I don't know, it's all so hard to understand. But it's easy for me to understand how happy I am with him, and being here. There are a lot of other people too.

He tells me he sends messengers up there once in a while, and he'll have one of them mail this to you. But there's no way you can answer, he says. Maybe I'll write again one of these days, but it's hard, not knowing how you're going to react to this. Maybe I will. Anyhow, I love you a lot, and hope you'll be happy. You can sell my car, by the way, and tell my aunts and uncles whatever you want. Maybe I'll write to them—why don't you say I ran away with a sheikh from Kuwait! No, that sounds stupid. Whatever you want. Take care of yourself, and think of me once in a while, especially on nights when there's no moon, he says, and maybe I'll hear you. Good-bye, honey.

Love,
Sunny.

The Infinite Tarot

Preface by Egon Ehrenreich, M.D.

In the course of psychiatric practice, it is inevitable that the analyst will from time to time meet, and be expected to treat, patients who are repulsive to himself. The Christian theologians understandingly distinguished between *detestatio*, a wilful, deliberate hatred of another mortal, and *abhominatio*, a marked yet unpremeditated dislike unfounded on specific grievance or quest for advantage. The former was deemed sinful, the latter a mere imperfection (unless it became a base for malicious action) to which flesh is mysteriously subject. In our days, with our sound grasp of etiology and the mechanisms of the unconscious, we perceive in *abhominatio* no mystery, and, if we have not yet judged it culpable, we have developed means to eradicate or palliate it, or at least to cope with its social and professional consequences.

When all that has been said, it remains to confess to the reader that I despised, detested and abominated young Jeffrey F from the first moment his post-acne'd face bleared in my office, from the very first time his small lazy body flopped sideways into my chair. He was to me more than a churlish, overfed, ignorant lout. He was the very paradigm of a generation of churlish, overfed, and ignorant louts that has vitiated the strength and post-war promise of my adopted country. Truly, it was hard for me to see him as an individual at all, so securely did he fit the pattern of his deplorable genotype.

He had been referred to me by his mother's brother, a colleague and sometime Go-partner of mine. He was well-aware of his nephew's unpleasant (to say the least!) character, and was eager to have that character modified without any contact with the family in general or himself in particular. The uncle's note had wryly proffered his diagnosis of the nephew's condition: delusions of creativity.

Jeffrey, it seemed, esteemed himself a jazz saxophonist. I made the mistake of asking him to perform for me. When the third visit came, he brought his instrument and played enthusiastically and mechanically, using one invariable formula: his selections were inevitably current hit songs, from which he would strip off whatever rock and roll or latino or (is it called?) country beat, and substitute a smooth, fox-trotty cantilena in which the melody, if any, was played in unadorned monotony. His heroes were salon orchestra leaders in the decade before my adopted country last fought my natural one. Of Charles Parker and Ornette Coleman and more recent artists of his instrument, young Jeffrey had this to say: "tone-deaf jigs."

The reader will wonder why I did not refuse his case, and refer him onward. The very strength of my *abhominatio* (I retain that difficult but morally comforting word) prevented that. I was egoistic enough to grasp Jeffrey's case as a challenge to my objectivity. To make a long story short, my objectivity was victorious, but my treatment was not.

Jeffrey seethed with resentments. His enemies were the Musicians' Union, all club owners, television producers, record company executives, Negro musicians, Dixieland jazzmen, players of Be-Bop, neo-Bop and Rock-a-Bop, Juilliard clarinetists, third stream composers, big bands, in-groups, the media, Rolling Stone, manufacturers here and abroad of reeds and mouthpieces, the new, reformed United States Department of Education and Culture, and an Austrian musicologist named Stute who had given him the one review he'd ever received. All these were against him. Jeffrey's loud and continuous vaunting of his "creative" musical faculties had gotten him no further in his profession than playing for the occasional neighborhood wedding with a pick-up band.

At the close of our fifth session, I broached to Jeffrey the familiar notion that creativity is often accompanied by an unsuspected latent gift in some other field. It seems that in all his life he had never consciously written, painted, drawn, carved,

molded clay, taken photographs, or built model railway scenery.
I urged him to try his hand at something else, just to sense out
the true largeness of his faculties. Why didn't he write a story,
perhaps from his own experience?

Three days later I received the narrative this brief account is
meant to preface. I read it with growing interest.

At our next interview, I questioned him closely about the
story. He told me it was in no way invented, but was "true-to-
life" in all details. When I questioned him about the curious
sexual menage that bulks so large in his story, he assured me
that the "three-way-pad" was normal in his group. Subsequent
researches on my part confirmed his description; a growing
number of louts (and lustresses, the new feminine of the word)
follow the pattern. To be fashionable, the boy must have a girl,
and the two of them together must have an "amy"—I suppose
from the French amie, "friend?"—a girl who is not a sexual
partner of either boy or girl, but who acts as confidante to the
girl and as sexual stimulator to the boy. She stimulates both by
reason of her untouchability (according to the code), and by the
deliberately and often outrageous lubricity of her behavior and
self-display. A girl who is the "amy" in one "threeness" will
very likely be the "girl" in another.

The actual denotation of mood, statement and response by
means of hummed or chanted pop tunes (where the correct lyrics of the given song = the message to be delivered or expressed)
I have already encountered in most adolescent patients to one
degree or another. It is an exacerbation of the spontaneous asso-
ciative processes that bodes little good for culture or society—specifically, because utterance ceases to be a *symbolic system*, and degenerates instead into a mere set of *signals*, and
those of the widest and least interesting distribution. This invol-
untary reduction of language capacity fills me with foreboding.

Several months of more or less adequate sessions followed
my rather favorable reception of my patient's story, though
more and more time tended to be spent in dereifying his para-
noid projections of cabals and conspiracies. My objectivity had
won for the young man a growing feeling of tolerance on my
part, trust on his, when an icy Tappan Zee Bridge put an end to

the existence of my subject, who is the author of the ensuing narrative, which I set before the public both for its sociological interest, and (its sole original virtue) for setting down on record for the first time, as far as I know, the theory of the Infinite Tarot, of which I had once, long ago, heard in my native Szeged.

—E.E.

"A Reading of the Cards"

Trudy has one of those dimpled tushies I hate to look at in the act so I tried to make Doreen give her up as our amy. But Dodo and Trudy have been together since music class and Bear's Rock, and Dodo says only Trudy can remember accurately the special words to all the songs they used to do there. All these girls from those private schools have all kinds of private lyrics, and when they're humming questions or answers or just hum-rapping, you never know if they really mean the real words or not. Like one time after we ate at that crappy Vietnamese place over on Avenue B Dodo hummed Like Baby I Don't Feel Too Good. That was the first time she brought Trudy along, and Trudy wet her pants laughing in that sick in way she has. Dodo and her kept humming little snatches of it back and forth all night. When we lurked back to the lotus and Trudy caught the Second Avenue home, Dodo told me that back in Syosset Hi, the song meant My Man's Is Just As Stiff As Wood. I hate that crap. We should stick to the real meaning of the songs.

This night we were at Dodo's, and all the while I was balling her, Trudy kept up that same monotonous wiggle over against the wall, left buttock up, left buttock down, right buttock up, right buttock down, just like they taught her in the South Indian dance class in Syosset. Then she'd dip her crotch and give another wiggle. If that's supposed to turn me on, it sure didn't. Most of the time I kept my eyes closed, but I feel bad when she's facing me, so I pretend to look at her. It's all I can do to keep it up, but Dodo won't let me say a word against her. Dodo is Joe Casiel's amy, and he tells me she's hot stuff for him and Lisa, so he probably has no idea of how awful Trudy is at the job. But I do feel sorry for the poor kid, since nobody's balling her now, and she's between Two's. Nobody seems to want to plug her in. She probably hopes she'll inherit me when Dodo gets married next June. That hip roll of hers, it's dumb to look at but it might not be so bad in the act. But she's such a dork.

So this night in particular I was really bored of watching her, so when I came I just lost interest and didn't want to do the After Bit at all. I wanted to get out. Dodo was cool, so we got dressed, and sure enough little Trundle-Oody came along tooly. I hummed Gimme A Chance in Doreen's ear, but Trudy caught it and started giggling. Must mean something dirty rimes with Pants.

We were going to go to the Hanoi Palace again, but Trudy kept lipping about this wonderful bla bla bla Gypsy place where they told fortunes and served a special Gypsy supper. Barf, I said, who stole the chicken? But Dodo was interested, she's been really into fortune-telling, wants to know what kind of husband she's going to draw come June. So we took a cab yet all the way up to the Black Candle Veil of the Future Restaurant. The meat is probably really squirrel.

I guess it used to be a Chinese restaurant before, cause the wallpaper had pagodas and little boats all over it. An old hag with henna hair, about as much a gypsy as my Aunt Estelle, came over and gave us menus, and set down a teakettle. Trudy recommended Combination No.4, Head of the Lion, which turned out to be hamburgers in barbeque sauce with fried potatoes swimming in grease. I got No. 1, slices of grey meat (too tough for squirrel) under the same sauce, same potatoes, same salad. Even the plates were those Chinese restaurant blue things, with more pagodas and more little boats, people in robes standing up in them pushing themselves along with poles. Dodo got the tuna melt.

We managed to get it down, and Trudy gobbled away, as usual. I hummed Lemme Inside You to Dodo, and she got her hand on me under the table. Trudy just kept shovelling. After a few more swallows I tried Let's Cut, Baby, Let's Cut, but Trudy came back at me with Tell Me What My Future, Conjure Man, and Doreen sang The Next Gotta Be Best. So we stuck it out for

dessert, which was brown sugar pudding with black flecks in it. I
hummed I Think I'll Die, and Dodo and Trudy really broke
up——they said it meant I Ate A Fly back in Syosset.

The tea was weird, and when we got round the pudding,
something dark and dirty crawled over, like a real Gypsy. Trudy
got all giggly, and the old lady clawed some leaves from the
kettle into each of our cups. She looked into them one eye at a
time. Mine first. She said I had a soft heart and was afraid of
women, but that I would soon meet one who would open my
eyes. She said I would have heart trouble later in life but
wouldn't tell me if she meant like love or like cardiac. "No
difference," she said. I started doing You're Handing Me A Load
Of but the girls didn't seem to notice, even when I pinched
Dodo's thigh.

Trudy came next, and the old bag looked a long time, then
she sighed and dumped the tea leaves out. "Tell me dream," she
shrieked at poor Trudy. After a lot of what do you mean and
back and forth and so on, Trudy finally got the idea. "Well,
there's this dream I have all the time. It's terribly frightening,
and I always wake up screaming when I have it. I have it all the
time, a couple of times a month." She turned pink and looked at
me for some reason before she went on. I hummed Hey, Say
Your Piece, and she got started again. "I'm walking down this
long yellow road, I mean it's like sand only not soft like sand,
and it's yellow. It's really more like a path, maybe as wide as the
sidewalk, and it goes on and on, I can never see to the end of it.
On one side is a high wall with no gate, the other side is a hedge.
Way over my head. I try to crawl under the hedge, every time,
but there are snakes under there, and they start coming out at
me, and I get up and run and run, and there's no place to hide, I
just have to keep running. I think somebody's coming after me."

I hummed Jewel Justice's new track That Ain't Me, but
Trudy probably hadn't seen it yet, cause she just looked at me
and then went on.

"I keep telling myself not to look around, but I get nervous-
er all the time, and finally I do look around. There isn't anybody
behind me, but all along the road there are funny shadows coming slowly after me, sometimes long skinny ones like snakes,

sometimes big clumsy shadows, all coming slow. It's the slowness that's so scary, I don't know why. I always panic then, and start to run and run again, and I keep running till I fall down. I never look around anymore. When I fall down I generally wake up. But I had this dream a couple of nights ago, right after we went to Bear Mountain on the hydrofoil, and this time when I fell down, one of the shadows got to my foot, it felt all dry and numb. I guess it was my foot falling asleep, cause it was asleep when I woke up."

The Gypsy lady seemed to be asleep herself, but when Trudy stopped, I gave a cough to wake her. The old girl said "Ver' important dream, you come back lunch tomorrow I tell you. Tonight I light black candle, you come back tomorrow lunch. Lunch." Then she looked into Doreen's cup and said, "Too dry now, dream take too long, leafs too dry now, I not can make them dance. Besides, for you the cards better. For you the cards. You want know about husband, cards are more better for. Two dollars."

I groaned, but Trudy insisted: "O do it, Dodo, it's worth it. She's wonderful with the cards—see, she knew you wanted to ask about a husband. And I'll pay for it, cause it was my idea to come here, and it's my fault the tea leaves got dry."

The old Gypsy waddled back to the kitchen to get what she needed. The minute she was out of earshot I laid it on the line for Dodo: "Look, Doreen, you remember Gloria, Epstein, who used to ball for your Jeff? Well, she knew how to read the Tarot cards, and she was amy for Pris and me for three months in senior year, and she taught us how to read them. I have a deck back home—you never asked me to read them for you. This bag lady just wants your money."

"Look, Greg, what can you buy for two dollars? What harm can it do? If you know so much about it, maybe you can learn more. Of if she's really a fake, you could show her up. I kind of want to see what she'll say."

The old woman was back so I had no chance to answer. She was carrying a big cardboard carton, painted dull black. Through the paint you could still see the Campbells Frozen Clam Chowder printing. The top of the box had a hole in it, like the ballot

box we used to use in class elections. It seemed to be full of
cards. She gave the box a good shake. "Now we see, now we
see."

The cute little 'Rican waitress came by and cleared off the
table. I told her to bring more tea, but she didn't hear me. The
old Gypsy woman spread out a piece of saran wrap on the table,
and began to pull cards one by one from the box, and laid them
face down in a circle right in front of Doreen.

"Hey, are those Tarot cards?"

"Gypsy cards, ver' old Gypsy cards."

"But are they Tarot cards?"

"Sure, sure."

She kept fishing cards out and putting them down until
there was a circle of twelve cards on the table. The backs of the
cards were greasy and dirty, they used to be blue. They had fish
on them, two of them, each one biting the tail of the other, and
they were bent like Sixty Nine. Between the fish was a black
guy's face, with his tongue hanging out.

The Gypsy turned over a card near the bottom of the circle
in front of Dodo. There were two blue birds on the card, one
upside down. "The Two of Doves," she announced. Then she
turned up the card above it. She was working back around the
circle, away from Dodo, counter-clockwise, so if the first card
was five o'clock, now she picked up four o'clock and turned it
over. This one had a hand on it, outlined in red. "The Ace of Left
Hands, ver' power."

"Hey, these aren't Tarot cards, I thought you said they were
Tarot cards!" I felt pretty good, and flashed a sneer over at Dodo,
who just looked down at her cards. "Well?"

"Sonny," the old woman whined, I hate being called sonny,
"sonny, what you know? These are not like tarrot cards you
know maybe. These are special new ancient Gypsy tarrot cards."

She faced up the next card, three o'clock. "The Three of
Sewing Machines," she said. "Watch out, news from far away."

"This is ridiculous! How can there be ancient Gypsy cards
with sewing machines on them? This is a fake."

The Gypsy had not really looked at me till now. She crank-
ed around in her chair and gave me an evil look.

"Sonny, this is ancient Gypsy tarrot. Your kind jewish maybe cathlic tarrot, are four signs, piece of wood, piece of tin, glass
of water, sharp knife. You think you know cards when you
know four piece of thing? *This* is Infini Tarrot, this is infini
ancient true tarrot. Two dollars I charge, not even silvier, I like
this poor girl goes around with dummy like you. You shut up
good, I read true ancient infini tarrot this poor girl. Nowhere else
America you find so true are cards. Is infini tarrot, ever'thing in
the world has a picture in it, ever' thing. If is a thing in the whole
world, tarrot has picture in it. Otherwise no can be in world if
not here, you understand? Now you shut up good or I take cards
home."

Dodo was humming Cool It Quick, so I let the joke ride.

The old witch turned them up faster now. The Five of
Bombs. The Seven of Left Hands. The King of Fountain Pens.
The Six of Binoculars. The Seven of Blue Jeans. The Ten of Cars.
The circle was opening up towards Doreen now. The Three of
Light Bulbs. The Nine of Small Rivers. The Four of Quartz.

The old woman reached down into the box again, and this
card she set down in the middle of the circle face up. "The
Mailman," she said. It was a good painting of a U.S. mailman, in
a purplish uniform, sort of a sad smile on his face, wearing the
winter cap with furry ear-laps, a big brown leather bag on his
shoulder. There was a fence behind him, with a mean-looking
dog trying to get its head between the fenceposts to bite the
mailman. In the background an old ranch house, with a hand
pulling back one of the picture window drapes slightly.

"I guess you're going to get a letter, Dodo." I wanted to keep
it light.

The Gypsy paid no attention to me, just looked at the cards
and sort of rocked back and forth on her behind.

"Oh, oh, no, this one not bring anything. This is one that
take thing away. Take thing from where is it, and bring it home
where it not go any more, never, never. You poor girl, you poor
girl, you not be care full."

I got pretty angry, because Doreen looked scared, and I
knew I'd be the one to have to calm her down. Sometimes it
takes all night if she really gets a jolt, and she dries up terribly.

Byebye bed if she got really turned off by this shit. I wondered if
Trudy had thought this stunt up to get into bed with me. I got up
to pay, but the spic chick wasn't in sight. "Come on. cut this
crap."

But Dodo kept gawking at the cards, and Trudy was putting
on a real act, even a tear dropping from the corner of her eye.

"Come *on,* do you hear me?"

The waitress showed up with the bill, with Cards $2.00 on
it after all the food. I didn't wait for Trudy to do what she said
she would, just paid the bill at the cashiers and came back to put
the half dollar tip down—right on the middle card. I grabbed
Doreen under the armpit and tugged her to her feet.

While we were getting out, the old woman was putting the
cards back in the box. We walked along Broadway a few minutes, very quiet. I felt bad that I'd made a scene. "What else did
she say while I was paying?"

Dodo didn't want to talk about it. Most of the way home I
had to hum with Trudy. Of all people. When Dodo stopped to
look in a window at some gold slacks, I pulled Trudy aside and
pumped her fast.

"Listen, what else did that bitch say?"

"I don't know, I don't know what it means, I think Doreen
is going to die!"

I hated the way she said Dor *Reen.*

"We're all going to die, you creep. What did she say?"

"I mean soon, Greg. Like Madame Riva was crying a little,
and kept saying how Doreen couldn't get out of it."

"Madame Riva shit. Did she actually say she was going to
die?"

"I guess not, but what else could it mean?"

"Bullshit."

Doreen came up and wanted to buy the gold lamé pants. I
figured what the hell, it might cheer her up, so we went in and
she tried them on. The creep had to go into the dressing booth
with her, of course. Dodo looked pretty good in them, I got to
admit, and I wanted her to wear them home, look good and save
time. But she wanted to change back into her sheath. When the
girls went back in, they pulled the wrong curtain back and there

was this other girl sitting there half naked, just sitting, bare chest, her hands in her lap, crying, tears all over her face.

When Dodo came back out she was OK again, and we got back to the shack in good spirits. I wanted some fun, after all this shit. but Dodo wanted to watch the box. So Trudy and I went into the kitchen and had a couple of beers. I was pissed off at Dodo, and didn't mind if she thought I was feeling up her amy, even if it is against the rules.

"Do you really have that dream, Trudgy?"

"Yes, Greg. Why would I lie about it?"

"I mean it sounds like one of those made-up ones you see on tv."

"Those dreams really happen, Greg. They get them from Case Histories."

"That what your Psych teacher told you?"

"Well, I mean, if you make up the dream yourself, it's the same as having it, isn't it? I mean when you're asleep, you're the one who makes up the dream, aren't you?"

I didn't say anything to that. She was leaning over putting cups into the automatic. That pinched-in behind kept wiggling. I'd like to take a hypodermic full of wax and jam it in, fill her out a little. Wouldn't be so bad if she didn't wear those white stretch pants.

"Here's your coffee, Greg, nice and strong, three sugars, no milk. Right?"

"Yeah, I see it. Thanks."

She sat down right next to me, so my right knee couldn't help pressing her thigh. What a cat she is.

"What's going to happen when one of those shadows really catches up with you? You ought to tell the doctor about that dream."

She didn't say anything. She knew I was just trying to scare her. After a while she hummed There's A Time To Be Afraid, just the part that goes

> *A girl is not the strongest thing*
> *but she keeps trying*

over and over.

"I think I'll try to find those cards Gloria gave me."

"Oh would you read them for me, Greg, please?"

I said I would, no sense in being mean to her all the time. Besides, it's best to keep changing the way I treat her.

After a little bit of a search, I found them in the bottom drawer of the chest, still wrapped up in an old letter of Jeff to Gloria, the way she gave them to me. The book was still there with them. I took the rubber band off, and opened the book on the table while I started thumbing the cards.

"See, Trudy, these are the real ones, the authentic ones."

She looked down on the pictures in the book.

I flipped the cards one by one. Swords, Cups, Sticks, Coins, Kings, Queens, Knights, Princesses. These were the real ones all right. There was that pregnant woman in green sitting in a garden, and I remembered that Dodo was a couple of days late. I wondered if it meant anything.

The Woman Who Had Five A's in Her Name

Did you know this about me when we met?) she wondered.
If I knew how to spell you I would walk, no I don't mean that, I
mean if I could spell, and the spell were you, and I kept things
clear, dear god let me keep them clear, why then I would be able
to be clear with you too and answer your questions, not the
questions meant to satisfy my ego-hunger for all the asking that
means all I could be asking, no, but really answering, the way a
woman answers a man or I answer a woman, let it now, this
moment, be you, no, but I mean really answer you) he thought.

Why should they not be clear?) she wondered. Why, what
species of confusion is he bringing to me?)

"I'm glad to see you again, there was so much the first time
. . . the path, the waterfall, the stone what was it, a ruined wall
or bridgehead, where we, sat, while your friend, the friendly shy
dark one, slithered down the slope and got to know the hither
streamside, while we, while we, sat beside each other on the
stone."

The feel of the stone) he thought. The feel of the stone
against our thighs and buttocks) he thought. That things have
feelings in flesh, that flesh answer unflesh, that is interesting,
strange, the feel of her, I remember reaching out and touching
her, lightly, lightly, her, where the top of the left buttock joined
the slope of the small of the back, there, her, as if I were touching the very possibility of her, anyone, sitting, on earth, being at
peace, I remember, what, what is she saying now? She isn't
asking a question, but, I have to answer, her, here) he thought.

"Yes," he said, "I remember. There was a strangeness to our
sitting there, then, I remember that, the feel of the stone . . . no,

74

I'm wandering, I mean there was a strangeness to us, the stone was ordinary, just touched us, pressed us, wait, no, forget about the stone, I mean we, we were strangely seated, in quiet there, on the stone, as you say, coping or, something left of the bridge, joining, now joining us, forgive me, I'm wandering, I mean, what was strange is that we were sitting and evidently just watching her go down towards the stream, and, and we weren't talking, though we were talking, but what, we were saying, what we were saying was really in aid of, saying this other thing, about how, I, I wanted, no, I mean I wasn't going down with her, I had refused to, and now, then I mean, I was sitting, mutely but alert, beside you. Because, simply, I wanted to make sure that contact of ours, so new, was not broken. And we could speak. Because all the while before you came out to visit, you, were asking questions, questions my whole life knew the answers to, though I may or may not have had the words of the answers in my mind to speak at any given time. Things are known." He said this to her now, hoping to be clear.

It seems she understood. They had been standing looking out the twelve-paned window, out over the ancient-looking fork in the road presided over by the dingy New England light that goes with winter, winter. She looked at him and then set her right knee on the edge of the bed, swiveled on her knee and let herself down on her right hip, half-lying, her right elbow pressed into the blue comforter-quilt.

Why is the road so old?) she thought. Why do we have to do this again and again and again? Why is it always done and never done, always begun and never finished? Is this our only road?) she wondered. By then he had mimicked her gesture and was lying in much the same way just behind her. She could feel his breath on her nape. Strangely, they were both still looking through the window, though this time only one of the roads could be seen, the one angling more or less sure and south. The tip of his tongue touched the back of her neck, just below the hairline, just once.

It is lovely skin and the fragrance of it comes up into my nostrils like a sacrifice Thracians made to a minor god) he thought. It is beautiful skin and a beautiful woman and how much we have to say to each other remains to be seen, to be said, to be seen, I do not know, I pray. Does the god pray back to his votaries on the ground: Make me real by your spilt wine and butchered rams, give me existence, only you can, be me with your songs and drunkenness and myrtle and mind-altering jive, your choric dancers, your stately bosoms held before you and the flesh of your teeth in perfect mouths, make me be!—is that what the god answers? Is that why I am kissing her now?) he thought.

"The fact that your tongue and lips feel good on me, and that my body shivers a little with some pleasure, does not keep me from asking: Why are you making love to me?" she asked.

"Am I doing that, isn't my body just talking to your body, body to body like two stones beside each other on a pasture, left by a glacier, no, it isn't like that, why, because there is feeling, feeling in me, and when there is feeling then it is something I am doing, feeling is what we do, so it is, really yes, as you say, I, this yes, this I, is, am, making love to you, just so, as you say, just now, and, as I, breathe in the fragrance, the German word is *Duft*, why do I think that, now, of your skin, the *Duft* of you, as in the simple, even mechanical, in-breathing, inspiration, literally, yes, just breathing you in, there, here is a responding in me, an elevation, a surge of those stones I was imagining, no, not stones, but surging, swelling towards you. What is this machine?"

It is a familiar machine indeed) she thought. So many times this machine has come towards her, always the same, never the same, come towards her, inside her, always welcome, never at home. Why. This is something not that they do) she thought. It is something we do) she thought. We do.

"It is what we do," she said.

"What, what?" he didn't understand, "oh, the machine, the machine is what we do, thank you," he understood, "you are sharing in this lust!"

He moved closer against her, and that wasn't what she meant at all, particularly, but she pressed back against him. It was always this moment, always this moment with everyone. It is the same with everyone) she thought. I am everyone) she thought. Everyone with everyone I am, I am, only what I am, that is what everyone is, the same, let it be] she imagined.

"This time, we, that we are here, together, this time, for once let it be as it really is, let us live this hour, this weekend or whatever, you and me, in sacred time, I mean I'm proposing that," he was speaking wildly, suddenly weakly, happily, off the top of his head, as ever, his best way, "proposing that we live in full mythic domain, dimension, that we be everything we are, that we say everything. Say everything. Reticence is wrong, reticence is, no, it isn't reticence I'm bothered by, but that, in you, in me, there is a speaking that doesn't speak. Just this once, this, time, let it speak. Let us say everything, do, do as our minds say, just this, not afraid, once!"

He was funny, what he was saying, mixed of obvious and wilfulness and wish, but right, he was right, he was saying what she was always saying, was he as brave as she was, it's so easy for men to be brave yet they're not, was he, as she is. What he is saying is what I'm always saying] she thought. But nobody ever does. What he's saying is how I am always wanting to be living, the full thing, the full thing, the life of being on earth the whole myth, the whole meaning, of, love and, past that, the gods, what are they, are they this moment, am I, now, exactly, a god because I hear him?] she wondered. Is a god the same as saying everything? And yet it's all about making love, his mouth muzzling my collar aside, muzzling along my skin, shiver, as if my vertebrae were outside my skin, his breath saying my skin, his hands opening my shirt, it's all about that, what he's saying is all about this, we're all all about this, nothing else. Why isn't there some other this, why isn't there something else?] she thought.

His hands indeed lifted her shirt pretty well away from her back, and his face pressed against her spine, the tip of his tongue working between the nodes of the vertebrae, saying the rosary down her back.

Why is it always all about just this?] she asked herself. And then, what is this about? It's all about sex but what is sex about? She said it out loud, What is sex about?, so he could hear. He did not desist from nuzzling her, nor did she insist that he do so. He spoke a word against her skin she couldn't make out, though she supposed that even now it was, somehow, making its way through her skin into the cavity of her body and would come in its own time to her heart, and she would know what the word is, was. Or would she? Does a heart know? Or would the word change as it moved from the mouth, the way a sound in music does, say, secular decay, the pitch changing as it dies, would the meaning, also, just that way, change as it passed through her. What did he say? "What did you say?"

"I said I'm talking to your body, it's what I mean, need, now, to say it straight, love is, isn't it, straight talk, didn't we always say? It is what I'm saying to you now."

But) she thought. But if love is straight talk what is myth, it isn't ordinary, it isn't just your mouth leaving a wet trail on my hip, snail trail, no, not disgusting, just there, just there but not myth, where is the meaning of what you're doing, to me, I mean, where is the meaning, to us, our meaning here, in this kiss) she asked herself, meaning to be asking him. But what is the point?) she relented. He wanted to be doing what he was doing, and he wanted to call what he was doing 'talking.' All right, then, she would listen, why not, that seemed only fair, if his will was all to bring himself to her, body, her and her body, or no, one, one bringing, implying or imposing a unity on the recipient, her, then her being quiet, relaxed even, would be nude to him, would be listening. That was listening, she was listening, she listened.

And as she lay there on his bed in his bedroom over the forking roads she thought she was hearing. If only the heart could hear as well as the skin does. Or does it. She was listening.

By now he was lifting the waistband of her slacks away, his left hand uncoupling the snap, pulling the slacks down over her hips. Every permission is a further permission. She did not know if she welcomed what was happening, but it was happening, and all the things she could have done to stop it or help it or encourage it were not being done. She was just listening, as he had asked her to be, asked by the fact of speaking. Speaking always asks hearing. What was he saying?

His tongue had worked along the sacral segments of the backbone, probing (is probing talking?) and had now found the gentle soft delve just where the buttocks began to swell on either side of this road he was following. Was he following his tongue?) she thought. Is that what language also is, one word following another, no, a person following the words, where do they go, what am I going to say, wouldn't it be wonderful if I could say everything, not everything but everything that comes into my mind or heart or skin or sex to say, let it speak, let me follow it, is that what language is?) she asked. Is that what language is, a man or woman following words that come before and lead on ever after, we are born and die and they are still speaking?) she asked again. We learn them from our mothers and from the street and there is no end to it.

How could love be different from that, following language from where it rises in me to where it flows in the world, feeling flowing as language between the banks that language knows but we can never see or guess, what are the boundaries of language, not what it can't tell but what keeps it telling, keeps it going, keeps it knowing? What shapes language that shapes us to follow?) she wanted to know.

A possible answer was pleasure.

A warm complexity was happening in her now, and a nervousness that distracted her from feeling what she was feeling as much as she wanted to feel it, since it was so much there to be felt. His tongue wetly massaged the region of the coccygeal ganglion, where the spine ended and the center of a person began, and this rich tumult of nerves lived. Gently enough he tumbled her forward so she lay fully on her belly, listening. A word is a myth?) she thought. Or the Greeks, we Greeks, have one word that comes to mean both, the word out of our mouth for good or ill, the words that mean what we say and all that we say is only as true as the moment of our saying it is, is that it, is that myth? Is it that myth itself is the only myth, I mean the fact of myth is itself the only mythology? The set of all sets) she guessed. The rimes bounced around in her head, not smoothly as his tongue, tongue, was slowly twirling on, that place. Then it was not. She felt the sudden absence of his attention, and a coolness where the wet was now evaporating in the dry bedroom air. Where was he? What was he saying when his tongue wasn't moving?

Then his tongue was touching her again. From the excited

receptors of her skin she could read clearly the the underside of the tongue now, smoother, wetter, was riding down the groove. If she looked over her shoulder she would see, she imagined, his head as if sinking into her. What are you saying? Why are you going there?) she wanted to know, but it was funny, somehow someone falling into me, is that what talking is? Is this what it means to mean something?

Now his tongue had come to the secret of her childhood, everyone's, the tender mystery, and pressed not so gently against it, then gentler, not gentle, gentle, not gentle, then began making little circular slow movements that, without in fact getting broader on the fact of her skin seemed to get bigger and bigger inside her, ripples on a pond, the circles grew wider and wider in her though the tongue kept up a steady slow round, around her. What was he saying? Was what she was feeling (what was she feeling?) what he was saying?) she wondered. Is what I hear what is spoken?) she wasn't sure.

His mind was clear and intent, no language in it except what he was speaking at this moment, the tongue to enter, decipher, taste, propose, renew, what am I doing?) he thought. All he knew was to go further. Gently now he began to press the tip of the tongue, made hard by so pressing, press between those small lips, entering, enter wetly, go far as, as far as, the muscles at the back of his tongue suddenly ached with strain as he pressed deep into her. He heard her gasp, whether with pleasure or at the frowardness of his caress he couldn't be sure, so pressed again, letting the tip of his tongue vibrate in the tight only slightly yielding constraint of what she, at that moment, simply was. Was there. She is here and I know her) he thought.

I am here and I am known) she thought.

On the third expedition of his tongue inside her, she felt him more swiftly slip out, and as he left, she felt a version of the same loss she was sometimes stricken by when a more usual member withdrew from its more usual lodging in her. From missing his tongue she knew she had enjoyed, is it enjoy, listened to, made something of, yes, understood his tongue, language, what he was saying, and understood how she was hearing. But his tongue was gone. He spoke out loud, and then the tongue darted back inside her.

"Look at this!" he had said, and the command made her get up and follow it; the thrusting tongue showed her where to go. She got up quickly and hurried down. A woman largely naked was stretched prone on the bed, her shirt bunched up around her shoulders, her slacks pulled down to her knees. A man was half kneeling on the floor, his head burrowing. She watched his head move a little, pressing forward, and at once knew the woman as herself, and could feel the pressure of his tongue inside her. She fell forward on him and passed through him, and found herself walking in the dark along the blade of his tongue as it pressed into her.

I am in my own body) she thought. I am in my own body twice, or once in two ways, I feel his tongue inside me, yet I am walking where he has called me, I am his scholar, obedient to language I move and feel, he called me here and that is language, this tongue of his, anybody's, calling. He's nobody special. Language is calling.

He was standing at her side now and took her hand. They began to walk ahead into the dark. Dark, but not so she couldn't see. They could see. Where is the light coming from?) she wanted to know. His hand held her, her right hand in his left, why, and she could still, still feel his tongue pressing in her. Yet his face beside her was calm, alert to this dusky place he could just barely see enough to travel through.

Was it right to make other language now?) she wondered. It is always right to make language) she decided. And what is other language, what other words? She wanted to make him talk, to see if when his mouth, here beside her, moved, she would feel it inside her where, even now, she could still clearly feel, even more and more feel, his tongue discussing its own meanings in her, pressing, caressing, what else did it know? What will happen when he speaks? If it stops down there, down here, do I want it to? It was hard for her to be here and have here also be there. Her mind was a clear mind, and she kept the distinctions clear: there is where I am feeling, and here is where I am being) she decided. Left it to later to wonder (what will happen when I feel?

"What will happen when you talk to me now?" She asked him out loud, and he answered the same way: "I have been talking to you all this while and still am talking. Don't you hear me?"

The words he spoke did not keep the sensation of his tongue from moving inside her. He was still there, and she with him, she was welcoming his tongue, she was taking him in even as she here was walking with him, she, she was, she was here when here is no different from there. She squeezed his hand with her hand and felt him squeeze back there, and there, and there and here.

He was so happy she squeezed his hand. It was a token, a return. The silence of her listening wasn't always enough to sustain him, though it should have been. Silence is enough to speak to. Silence is permission enough for any language. Any mouth. Silence is hearing enough, I should believe) he thought. I have lived in the adequacy of what does not speak, does not answer and does not ask. It is good, so good, of her, this much, to answer. And by so doing, squeezing, raise other questions. The spelling of her name, for example, the multiplicity of instances, so few letters so many words, an alphabet makes so many things possible. All the instances that seem to be one self. A name. So many things possible, but not all things. Not this—and he pressed deep inside her as they walked.

"I know where we are, where you told me to come, but what does it mean that we are here, I mean here this way we are now."

"You mean here together?"

"No, here as we are. Two people walking inside one of them. Because the other is doing something still, I feel you in me still, how do you do it, no, I mean, here we are. Where is this place now, I mean now that we're here? Is it different from where you're talking, your tongue is, there?"

"I don't know," he said. "I think we're wherever we've talked our way to. I know I am inside you, some, and want to be further, I want to be further than any tongue can reach."

Further than language can go?) she wondered. He doesn't know) she thought. He doesn't know and I don't really want him for knowing. I thought I did and he thought that is who he was, is, and how he wanted to be wanted, someone who knows or could anyhow find out, and bring me there, that isn't it at all. He doesn't know and I don't care. it's not all about knowing. Not knowing, but something else. And not being, either. What is it that is neither knowing nor being?) she wanted to know.

"What is it that is not knowing and is not being?"

He didn't know. Feeling? Going? Each of those is beautiful, sinister, fatal, even, since feeling always stops. Even pain doesn't last forever. And going comes to an end and is just gone. Once he had said I feel so sad, and someone had said, Don't worry, that's only a feeling.

"I don't know," he said, "let me ask you a question. Maybe it's really the same question: what is it that is not feeling, and is not going?"

A name! a name is the answer) she thought. A name knows nothing, and doesn't exist except by imputation. It doesn't feel and doesn't go and doesn't come.

"A name," she said.

"A name," he repeated, wondering. "I don't know what a name is, so maybe that's the right answer. Maybe we're walking along in your name. How do you spell you? How are we going? Is this our alphabet? A is everything we say? The light brown clothes I dismember for you, whatever you lay aside? The avenue we walk on? I too want to know where we are."

"A is for are, you are, and A is for am, I am, and we are, all the way home. We move together, I don't know why, we are in each other, feeling, seeming to go, and . . . "

"A is for and!"

They were learning how to spell her name. There are so many ways and so few letters. That is why spelling is so difficult, why again and again we must use the same few things, the same few poor little ideas. Spelling is the first science, the hardest of them all. It is whatever they must go.

So hand in hand through the only alphabet they took their way.

Lecture on Cadmium

Suppose the dreamer finds himself required to address a learned assembly on a subject not of his own choosing. The assigned topic, let us say, is cadmium. The dreamer is not informed of this topic until the very moment it is announced to the audience by the gowned personage who has guided the dreamer to the rostrum from a dark hallway, and who now speaks the formalities of introducing the dreamer by name to the select assembly. The dreamer does not even know where he has been, much less where he is now, this place in which he stands and must presently speak. Above all, he knows nothing of his audience, their interests, preparation, skills. As the introductory remarks draw to their close, the dreamer finds himself moving reluctantly but steadily toward the podium.

There are no notes on the sloping plastic lectern; nonetheless, the dreamer turns the reading-light on. He opens his mouth to speak.

Cadmium is a heavy metal, source of vivid pigments he has admired in oil paintings, yellow deep enough almost to be orange, bright enough for sunshine, and intense Chinese red without the least admixture of blue or purple—true reds clean as fire. In his cupboard he thinks is a set of dinner plates and bowls from the Orient, perhaps Korea, metal, smooth, made he guesses from a cadmium-red enamel ware, bought years ago on a wharf in San Francisco. He remembers out loud that a friend not ignorant of medicine had warned that cadmium is released into hot food and into the eaters of food from such dinnerware, and slowly builds up toxic levels in the organism. This effect is irreversible. The audience does not stir.

84

For cadmium, like all the heavy metals, is poisonous to men and animals. Lead. Arsenic. Thallium. Gold. Interesting, he thinks the audience will find it, that all humans (except, it is said, the Andaman Islanders) sprinkle their food with chloride crystals of the lighter metals, sodium if they can get it, or potassium. But no one eats the heavy metals, except in Chinese fairy tales of alchemists and Taoist adepts who learn how to live on earth so that it turns imperceptibly into heaven. They eat pills of quicksilver. Cinnabar, immortality.

The dreamer is talking off, of course, the top of his head. His eyes move with anxiety over the unforthcoming faces of his listeners. He sees nothing to encourage or dismay him. They are just listening.

There is no clear demographic preponderance before him, no sign he can read. Young are there, with old; white with black and oriental, female with male. He talks. That is all he can do. And, he feels with a sudden stirring of something like comfort, that is all he is asked to do.

Cadmium yellow as a name always reminds him of crome yellow, a color he does not know so well, lemonier it is, he fancies, paler, more skeptical. Huxley's novel he'd read as a boy, when he loved that earthly paradise of clever prattle and free sex Huxley made so plausible the dreamer went on for years looking for it in his earthly life, and sometimes found. But he can't remember if it's Crome or chrome, from the painter's name or from chromium, isn't that green? Heavy metal, additive of steel. Chrome steel, vanadium steel. Pour charcoal dust into molten iron, the Arabs did, the single deed that made them Arab, charcoal and the Kor'an conquered half the world, charcoal dust into molten iron, cool, a million diamond crystals form, and the metal hardens to be steel. This is how it is. History is chemistry. Other metals can metal in too. Fuse. Any? Alloys and adventures. A word in the dictionary, lusting for others of its kind.

Now if we add crystals of sublimed cadmium to molten copper, we achieve a dichroic-lustered peculiar metal whose ardent rubitude belies the narcoleptic properties of acidic fruit-juices drunk from vessels cast from it. And is not asparagus itself especially rich in cadmium? Or mushrooms, or bananas? How little the dreamer knows.

How little we know by knowing, without quotation. Cadmium must be named for Cadmus the dragon-slayer, founder of Thebes, who sowed the dragon's teeth and reaped sturdy warriors. Late in life he underwent a non-surgical transformation from human to serpent nature, and with his wife, similarly reconstituted, writhed off into exile, no worse that the rest of us. In Cadmus' name, which the Greeks of the isthmus would have spelled *Qadmos*, we read a reminder of the Hebrew All-man *Adam Qadmon*, the primordial person —*purusa*—whose body is our whole humanity of all times, and whose dream is our history, our cosmos. When he stretches out his arms, his hands reach six inches past the edges of the universe.

But cadmium is not the primal metal, is it. That must be aluminum, why, for all its recency, alumina most common of, Napoleon III's helmet too, why value that which is everywhere? Everywhere but here. Cadmium sounds, doesn't it, like cambium, the yellow also sheath of life in living trees, beneath the woody bark. The golden sheath. Greeks and North Italian painters, cadmium unknown to them. Yet they lived in the world. Bleak yellow of Etna. Vesuvius. Sulphur.

As his sentences grow shorter, the distance between the topic of each sentence and the next grows longer—this is the Ratio of Morpheus, the desperate gloomy leaps a dimming mind makes while on its way from waking to sleeping, or from dream to that dreamless sleep at the bottom of the world, into which the dreamer now wordlessly floats from the podium without a single sign ever being given of how his audience has reacted to his forever inconclusive discourse.

2

A Line of Sight

CHAPTER I

I live in an old house that has no address.[1] The house is dark most days. Years ago it had a name,[2] taken from the two lime trees that block the afternoon sun from the front windows, trees much sought by bees in May and June. Tea is made from the flowers.[3]

Especially at the foot of the stairs it is dark, bottom of a dry well. On the wall above the last few treads is a large map of the Kingdom of Bhutan (Druk Yul), showing in monochrome relief the ranges and valleys and waystations. In the uncertain light that at times falls on this map from the opposite room, the tan spread of Druk Yul (isolated from the uncolored surround, India, China, Tibet) sometimes resembles a large cookie,[4] at other times a fallen leaf, which before withering rumpled into crests and gorges.

In one corner of the map there is a smaller replica, in outline, of the map itself. This diagram is called a Reliability Index, and shows sector by sector the confidence, expressed in percentages,[5] that the viewer can feel in the information sketched or verbalized in the large map. It is to be wished that every map conceded in such a way the inevitable inadvertency of its parts.

To the left of the map, and somewhat above it, there is a fierce grinning bright polychrome demon mask of unspecified origin, clearly enough the product of some tantric intelligence of the mountains. Bhutan. Tibet. Believers identify the mask as the face of an adept holding back his semen, resorbing his orgasm, swallowing the world. The face is the brightest object in the hall at the foot of the stairs.

89

Note 1: no address. A road, but no street. A street, but no number. Off east, beyond the sumac and the hill, the loosestrife and the small marsh anxious these nights with singing frogs, there is a crossroads where the highway runs fast past the almost unseeable entrance of a road whose name is like mine—but that's beyond 9G, beyond time, beyond the Ennead that stands this side of the Dodecad—that's a region between the Nine and the Zodiac, in which no fixed knowledge is. No steady knowing. Nine Gods look up and worship, Twelve look down and see me standing there, afraid as any four-year old to cross the blazing highway. Corner of the Dog. Nine Gods. Turn west with me. And then the house, with no address, too close to the Post Office to need one, just two houses down towards the stream. Known by name. This is the center of a vast invisible city; yesterday as we drove along, I saw a broken pump, its handle rusted, pointing towards the mountains. And saw the ultimate city, now only a dream, inhering in that space. Certainly it will have post offices and streets among its lily pools and tiger walks; I am less sure it will have numbers. No address except the name of the city, The City, and the mail gets there. When I first moved to this town, I computed that by the grid of my city down the river, I lived on 2097th Street, West 2097th St. But that city is no longer anybody's system. The grid is more spacious now, builds up as well as out, comprises the nearer stars, has its root in water.

Note 2: a name. Erwin Smith the Postmaster lived in the house around the turn of the century, and called the place Lindenwood, from the two in front, one at the side, saplings all round. The tree is Schubert's *Lindenbaum,* an aching song of nostalgia that summoned Hans Castorp back into the bourgeois world from the bourgeois dreamworld up Davos. I don't know much about Erwin Smith, but pieces of hardware from the original house turn up in other houses round about. A characteristic door-hinge. A hasp.

The house has a name. When John Navins still kept the old Barrytown Post Office by the unused depot on the river, I found in his postcard rack a view of this very house, E. Smith's Lindenwood. I bought it for a penny (the same coin that would, in its time, have been enough postage to send it, say, to Helen's Great Aunt Malcha, that beautiful woman, who carried her best dishes from Poland to Texas in the late eighties—my card would have caught her in St. Louis, perhaps around the time of the Exposition). A search in Navin's shop turned up a brown-wrapped parcel of several hundred such cards, which I bought almost all of, leaving some for the unlikely traveler who might want some evidence of having spent one day in his busy life at the Three Corners, beside the stream Metambesen, under Cedar Hill, primal Annandale.

Note 3: flowers. Tilleul, lindenflower tea—the French are very fond of this, and the Germans only a little less so—no doubt it is their bee-natures coming to expression. Tilleul is likely the most popular *tisane* or herbal infusion, or shares the summit perhaps with chamomile (from which I once rolled myself a very interesting cigarette, on Bank Street, to decongest—successfully—my tight chest from a New York midwinter catarrh, while Diane Wakoski talked about Beethoven, and in the other room La Monte Young was writing a long detailed letter to Diter Rot in very black ink). Linden tea I have never tasted. Absurd to buy, with all the flowers we have each spring. I promise myself one year I'll gather some flowers and brew. But I no longer believe our health depends on herbs, and the branches of the big trees are a little bit above the reach of my naked arm.

Note 4: a large cookie. As one sits and hears the last large sumptuous measures of Richard Strauss's *Capriccio,* his last opera, written and performed (in the recording heard now) while the world was burning down around him, and no countesses ever again would read sonnets, or hum them aloud before the mirror late late after a desultory party, and no woman would ever again try to make up her mind, and for all I know, no mirror ever again would stand clear on a wall, calm in its gilt oval (that shape in which a woman sees herself most truly), it is false or feeble to think of food. Yet there are times, especially at night, when the house seems to be alive with a midnight appetite, an astral Dagwood planning strata of unlikely foods, a sweaty old rich Rossini turning from music to, what? What would Rossini have eaten late at night, when the sky was too bright with stars, too sculptural with cloud, too clever with nightingales, for him to go to bed, however pretty his companion or compliant nurse, what would he eat, while his kidneys ached and the moon sashayed across what he already knew must be one of the last lovely spring midnights of his life? Here again the thought of food is a blunder, fart of a woodnymph pursued. But what would he eat? Would he tinkle a bell, and a cadre of diligent, unsurprised servants fall into *sorbet* formation, or pull a mousse providently beforehand from the ferns around the ice-block in the double-doored chest? After the truffles and gooseliver and cockscombs at dinner, what would pacify the, not hunger, truly, the *need,* a pure spiritual need it may be, yes, Rossini's utter desperate agonizing need to take into himself now before sleep or love or dying, just one more morsel of this after all adorable cosmos. He is silent as he watches them carry first a table, then a silver tray with Something on it across the dark lawn. We shall not stay to see him lift the cover.

In this house some similar tendency, less elegant, less poignant, for our sun will never fall from the sky, true?, it's always here, yes?, always as it is now, supreme and ordinary, forever, ewig, ja?, some similar nudge of appetite troubles the hours between midnight and sleep. What will it be? Not then the earnestness of cheese and oil and garlic and bread. A cookie, a biscuit, something heavy, crumbly as earth, dry, not juicy, not sweet, not very sweet, no creamy inwards, no chocolate, understood?, a dry fine halfsweet crumbly cookie, no slimy cakes, no deceptive froth or teeth-aching icing, just the fine dry halfsweet, less than halfsweet cookie. That comes to mind some rare nights, when Bhutan becomes the half of an immense peanut butter cookie, say. But then a voice from the hallway cries: Man! Do not eat your world! Man! Man! Man!

Note 5: expressed in percentages. In fact the diagram in question reveals upon inspection only the alternatives: Good. Fair. Poor, distributed over the gradients. Memory said otherwise, and must have its little say, for fear of what She will do if balked of her constant ameliorative urge: Improve the Past, Improve the Past, Begin by Improving the Present, etc. A man who constantly corrects his memory may find himself eaten by tigers or bitten by scorpions, carried by eagles, trampled by bulls, disliked by other men—no pedant worse than the pedant of inner experience. An accurate memory is needed only when one is going somewhere, n'est-ce pas? Or has been somewhere. The intense static beauty of these nights needs no more memory than a dog has, between one bite and the next. Here it is.

Percentages have the advantage of being, by definition, relations to that definable Hundred (old Satem-Centum), a number in historical times roughly between 92 and 120, with a tendency for the higher sum to be operative in more northerly climes (Iceland, Wessex, Trondheim). Whereas in Hebrew the number Hundred is exactly equal to 10^2, and is spelled exclusively by the ten successive *yods* emitted from Nowhere which implanted the Tree in whose branches, now in sun, now in shadow, we have for a while the right to live.

On the other hand, it was always peculiarly irritating to my father to hear any price over ninety dollars described as, for instance, ninety-four ninety-eight. He would insist, with some show of reason, that for such sums we must say, A Hundred Dollars, and get it over with. In this I felt an honesty of mind, anxious to hear the truth however horrid, so anxious in fact that it preferred, after endless years of pain, truth plainly swollen with trouble to truth corseted and faking a smile as it puffs its way in. Let's hear the worst, he'd say.

It is my hope that Pradyumna P. Karan, cartographer of the Druk Yul map, leaned similarly to exaggerate the painful, and that his "Poor" is a cautious way of saying fairly reliable. But I fear the reality is even worse than the disclaimer. Was it a lake or a mountain? I hear him thinking, Was the government bungalow on the yang or the yin side of the hill, I must have written it down somewhere, is this the road to the airport or the path infested with giant leeches? is this little dot the leprosarium or the monastery? is that a cliff or a deer park, a forest or glacier, a pit or a pinnacle? There are no answers, there must be no answers, he has never been there, no one has ever been there. Most maps of this state do not show the town in which this house stands. There is a bridge over a river with an Indian name (Sepascot?), a small dam, a pool of deep quiet water dammed, apple trees, many locust trees, the kind of alder called red willow, whose inner bark is smoked. It is a place only real, without fame, without maps. No one has ever been here before.

CHAPTER II

The bond between the mountain and the map is color, and color is what is hardest in the dark house. The great dark lime trees keep back the road and the light. There are days in June when the year's not too wet that the bees themselves are frequent enough to break the light, noticeably dim it with their elaborate speculative lacework at the window. The light must come from the room through the archway into the hall at the foot of the stairs. In the hall there the map of Bhutan is large, and under it a map of Yucatan[1] is small but colorful, with tiny pictures of temples and deities marking the sites. In that specific sense, the god was flayed in the hallway, in halflight, or in the evening ugly yellow glare of the three overhead bulbs, Uxmal was built.

These places are important as separations.

Below the tantric mask is a simple drawing of two mature bears walking side by side across a sketchy field. Their noses tend towards Bhutan, but between them and that fanciful goal are two objects, mounted on the lintelpost[2] itself: a circuitboard from a very early computer, handsome and abstracted from all function, a stuffed circuit, considered as an artifact for the eyes to admire. Below that, a clear snapshot of a much-loved cat who died at one veterinarian's from an obscure disease contracted while he was being boarded at another, shortly after we came back from Mexico. Below the bears is a Nying-ma yantra, a diagram we acquired in California, in the Tibetan language. We have never been practically in Tibet, and can observe the mandala without a specific sense of loss.

Note 1: Yucatan. The neighborhood has a number of spiritual links with Yucatan, and at least one unpublicized telluric *nadi* or geo-astral vein unites the two terrains. Stephens, the first anglo into Maya country, brought back from the jungle many chests of Yucatecan antiquities; these he stored with his friend John C. Cruger, who lived on his (almost-) island up the road and river half a mile. In a local library, there's a first edition of *Incidents of Travel in Yucatan* inscribed by the author "to my friend John C. Cruger." Only ruins, or strictly speaking, ruins of ruins, are still to be found on Cruger's Island (though there is a wonderful rock formation shaped like two breasts on one chest—the Breasts of the Goddess An or Danu or Donu, for whom this district is named—one can climb between the breasts and sit there nestled, look out on the river, dabble feet in it if the tide's right). They say that Cruger's Stephens' antiquities were later floated on a barge downriver to form the nucleus of the Meso-American collection at the Brooklyn Museum, close to which I used to live, and in the library of which I first read Stephens—knowing none of all this. But my ignorance did not keep me from living a dozen years (or more?) in this northernmost outpost of the Mayan Empire, a ruin like the rest, surrounded by dense thickets and a quiet swamp with very black water.

Note 2: lintelpost. At one time, after the house was built, archways were cut, facing each other, admitting from the hall to the music room at the right, the study at the left. Years after that, both arches were reduced, by means of chipboard stretching from the original lintel to a new false doorway in which a cheap new panel-less door was hung. Two isolated rooms were thus formed with a hall between them. At the time of our entrance to the house, the arch to the music room we caused to be restored, leaving the study able to be shut off by its flimsy door from the hall. So it is on the chipboard panel between the adventitious doorway and the original lintel of the square arch that certain of the items are mounted to which attention has here been called: the yantra, the bear couple, the mask.

Though it forms no proper part of this account, the east lintel of the restored archway into the music room does constitute in fact the defining edge or obstacle by which the line of sight is bounded on the southeast. It is thus strictly of marginal interest, the gutter of this left-hand page these remarks propose to read. Yet the same lintel, clearly not the lintel in the text proper, but the one facing it, closer to the piano, closer to the yellow chair—that lintel was for several years one of the two foci by which the elliptical presence of the Ghost Dog made itself known. The ellipse in question extended from several feet into the hallway and music room up, at an angle we guessed to be 45°, to the landing at the top of the staircase. The Ghost Dog never appeared elsewhere, but for years could be seen frequently at the head of the stairs, or abruptly wheeling round the lintelpost downstairs. Even now, the Ghost Dog is sometimes seen in the latter, or lower, location, as if the slope of his presence were also a slope or declivity in time, the lower always later, the lower always later.

Since the installation of the Weber piano, with the découpage

panel front, and the A's that stick in several octaves when the weather
is damp, as it so often is, the free movement of the spectre has evidently been limited; the piano abuts on the lintel, and thus occupies
the area his ghost paws and muzzle invaded on those typical nights
when he would calmly and unmenacingly come through the arch and
disappear.

CHAPTER III

The point is, that these objects are not alone in the hall, by any means, but are the ones that can be seen, wholly or in part, from the yellow armchair[1] that stands at the end of the music room[2], close to the one window the sun reaches, but divided from window and sun by a square small table covered with cactuses, some living, some questionable, some dead. The cactuses have not stood there for a full year yet, by any means, so it is uncertain whether in warmer weather they will be moved to one of the porches, there to be at the mercy of possums and cats and raccoons, or whether they will be allowed to remain at the safer sunny window, at the expense of the chair which will thus be unable to come close to the window when need arises in the heavy heat[3] of a river summer.

Walls call for the futile and the dead. Unvisited kingdom, dead cat, unplugged-in circuit, unacted mandala no less a circuit diagram of an essential but incomprehensible process. Everything is there but an oil painting to complete the taxidermic array. We hang our dead upon the walls , and dare the sun to shine thereon. Taxidermy = to arrange the skin: to decorate the surface. More honest the stuffed owl in the study, the stuffed blue kingfisher out of sight (though in the hall) around the corner, on top of the old escritoire.[4] But the gaudy demon mask, of papier-mâché formed soggy from minced up manuscripts or codes of statutes or Gujerat newspapers, gilded now and painted in red and blue, toothed, muscled, gasps in the light. It is the brightest object by daylight or candlelight. The light knows how to find it. The face is doing something.

Note 1: yellow armchair. I first met S.K. (the initials are curiously enough the same as my father's) when he and his first wife had just separated. I never knew her, except for whatever inferences I might have chosen to make from the furnishings of the house she'd just abandoned. I did not choose to make any inferences at all, and was content to know S. in his present tense, a learned, various, skillful man. After some years, he met and married an extremely handsome woman Helen and I had known slightly in another set of connections. Into our knowledge of S., then, came his new wife, D. Time passed, and at length D. began to make just such observations as I had omitted. She perceived her house full of relics of this (to all of us except S.) unknown and not clearly interesting earlier lady. Soon enough then, these offensive objects started leaving the house. S. and D. were kind enough to think of us, and passed along three occasional tables surfaced with tooled leather, a sofa and armchair matched in yellow relief upholstery, and a Simmons high-quality bed. We had never bought furniture, and these gifts, while substantial and useful, were not after all surprising, since things have a way of migrating (as another friend, C., would say) towards our house. To put it another way, I have never seen a house so rich with arrivals. A dim historical sense persuades me to confess that my cigarettes and lackadaisical habits soon did for the leather tops of the tables. The sofa went on the porch (books are stacked on it, in cartons, waiting to go. Where?). The armchair is by the window. For my present purposes (if these discursions may so be dignified), this chair is important. For one thing, it is the one armchair in the house in which I'm comfortable. I can sit in it as long as I like, write in my notebook, read lovely Barbara Shapiro's biography of the great John Wilkins, listen to Wagner, listen to Helen playing Ravel at the piano, or just think about women, or about how I'm 38 years old and people still give me chairs. But the most important thing about the chair is that at times I sit in it and see nothing except what is directly in front of me, a single line of sight these notes attempt to deliver to a world hungrier for them than it probably knows. Of all things, it needs most to look one way with all its eyes. As for the bed, we'll sleep in it tonight.

Note 2: music room. Each day the scant sky light (not skylight) enters the room from the west. For a long time the room was a living room or sitting room. People came and sat on the long yellow sofa, the yellow armchair, the blue bentwood armchair, hassocks, folding steel chairs with curved wooden seats, the piano stool. But they stayed too long and said too little. As time passed, the room turned its space into accommodation for piano and scores, records and tapes and the machines to play them, a radio that could always reach the old city 100 miles away, and on some rare days (low cloud cover, minimal solar flare activity, a little wet coming down) could pick out the older city 200 miles over the mysterious oldest mountains east. So the room filled with different sonorities now, no longer the uneager implicit voices of young people confessing their desires or pressing urgently, shark-fashion, their omnivorous need for omnivorous attention, no longer the louder yelps of friends faltering towards middle-age full of negativity and suspicion, no longer the paranoiac drones of distant anthologies or local politics. Now the room was fuller with sound, sadder in a way not to have people squatting all over it, but not much lost, maybe not much lost. The room, that room, was never meant to be a khan or caravanserai—the sad ugliness of talk in that room came, as much as anything, from the room itself, from the sweet sense of snug enclosure it gave the visitor, the comfort of knowing he was held and cherished; in that maternal power, all the locked in shittiness and suppressed whine corpse-floated to the surface. So men and women who outside (or even in another room) (any other room?) laughed and held their masks in place and acted as if they had control of their own, if not lives, then at least responses-to-their-lives, in this room turned infants. Infans = unable to speak. Infants who pretended to talk, while all the while their hearts dripped down huge round american beauty baby tears that it could not be "like this all the time," that they were here, held and o.k., and in their hearts they hated the enclosure, fouled the room with their mental diaperings, blatted, bleated, left at late hours when the night was too far gone for anything but sour. In the morning, their dead cigarettes and unfinished drinks (identical with those to be detected, at that hour, anywhere, in any unloved, room in, this world) were pedestals for dust and demons. Every morning the room had to be ritually cleansed, incense lit, blinds opened, windows raised—the sorrow lasted. *These were not people* who sat here while the constellations rose and set, who complained and fantasized and went away. They did not know that this house was a journey. They took it for a rest. So the room excluded them at last, cast out the sofa and the music began.

Note 3: heavy heat. It is said that last year there was rain every day in the month of June. The summer altogether was agreeable to us when we came home after a year and a day, or a year to the day, allowing for leap-year. Only during our first week in the house, the house still foreign, smoked with strangeness, a dirty window, was there heavy heat. Then we dragged the bed (the former guestbed—we were camping in the house still) over to the west window and found after midnight most of that week enough wafted air to sleep by—except for one night when I roamed through the house and wrote to no purpose perched at the high writing table—no, not there, that had not yet been brought out of the store-room—so it was downstairs, at the kitchen table, the study still too strange to repossess. Then and a month later three days of heat. The summer was as I loved it, cold, wet, unpredictable, with days blazing like a polished shield on a pebble beach, quenched suddenly by a rip tide—*aither* days I called them, knowing the word of Greek for the upper air, where fire lives that does not burn, but moves all things in brightness. Then autumn came early, cold days of October, but the winter was mild, so mild that I only recall a few days of being cold, a few days of snow, the way a man healthy all his life might recall in age a few days of childhood sickness, precious for the difference.

A lovely rain. Falling now on Annandale after a warm March day. Spring frogs on both sides of the bridge, both sides of the house. Spruce wet tips, gnarl of oak and locust, smooth of maple, bare against the close sky. Cars parked not far away, they glisten clean or muddy in the passing light of other cars. Violet light in the woods where a woman with a deep voice in a new house bathes her flowers all night in false sunlight, mild. A distraction most of the year, allowable tonight seen through the lovely rain.

Note 4: escritoire. This family heirloom or Twentyish "secretary" stands of course out of sight, but it has stood near me since my earliest memories. Perhaps in its grimly pitted and scarred way, it is my memory. Every year or two, the urn-turned wooden finial that surmounts the center of the top must be jammed down in place, the original nails still intact, never yet making perfect contact. It stood in the living room of the house I was born towards, a room that patterns still my understanding of such things as carpets and sofas, vases and sunlight. The old story. The secretary (as it was always called) has four drawers, largely unhandled of its onetime bronze fittings, a yawning gap (Ginnungagap) above the drawers in which a cubbyhole-pigeonhole console fits, and a glass-fronted wooden-fretworked double-doored bookcase above that. The cubbyholes are gone now into another room, and the glass doors are locked with an omnipurpose mock-antique barrel-key not at the moment in hand. It will turn up. In the bookcase section is my meager gathering of old books and leather-bound trophies; the oldest is the editio princeps in Greek and Latin of Aristotle's works (Lyons, 1597), the sleekest an eighteenth-century vellum of Theocritus, the loveliest Baskerville's octavo printing of Catullus. The name "secretary," though, continues to haunt me. From the earliest times I imagined concealed within the veneered processes of this most angular desk a feminine presence lurking, coeval not with the wood but with the joining, a sort of loving easy flapper, late Friday afternoon, office party, Thorne Smith novel. Her clothes are insubstantial as her thoughts, but both are tender, playful, warm. She will not marry the boss because in the deepest world she is the Boss; for all the fragility Fitzgerald and his crowd found in her, to me she is most durable, surely more lasting than the bronze that would have locked her in. The key is lost, and she moves freely in and out, not I suppose of the furniture itself, but of the name "secretary," a name whose ambiguity owes perhaps something to the gin-scented hebephrenia of the earlier century. Nymph. Nymph whose svelte contours were implicit in the earliest Night from which Eros himself came, a spectre of her loveliness, to her forever returning, turning. Even as from the woman's dream and woman's *space* the first man arose, perhaps to do her work, perhaps to serve her.

CHAPTER IV

Because of man's sins, he perceives the sphere as a circle. Reflected from its convexity, the items of the wall and hall arrange themselves, maps and beasts and masks, thermostat[1] and architecture. The lintel says: This is where the wall ends, or the door begins. Or the door ends, and no man can pass by. Because of his sins. In the sphere of sight, every object becomes a surface, a surface becomes a word. The word, because of his sins, wanders down the centuries between what we laughably call its root and what we, half-ashamed, half-hopeful, describe as its obsolescence. The word wanders, meaning only one thing to him at a time. Because of his sins. Sin, says Clement, is inadvertency.

Lost word?[2] Every one is. Lost word, when the pale sunlight through the unclean window gasps the last shadows of dimensional things? Lost word stuffed between the cracks of a broken pane, to keep the wind out. But there is little wind most weeks, and the storm-windows contrive a more sophisticated protection. And what was the word?

Note 1: thermostat. Set at 62° winter days, 59°–60° winter nights when the incident light of the hallway allows less accurate knowledge of the dial. Very cold days, set for a few hours at 66° and let it be. To change the setting, it is necessary to hunch over and peer into the bronze box, careful not to get between it and the light, and then twirl the milled knob with the right hand until a little blue interior spark flickers to mark a change of state. Immediately a roar begins in the furnace room below, or else cuts out. In less than a minute, water is gurgling subtly in the radiators, either perking up or coming to rest. Heat, anciently loving to rise, climbs all day to the upper story and lies in wait for the sleepy householder. Often it is stifling at the head of the stairs, the long hall to the bedroom lined with books and maps. By the doorless doorway, the heat is gentler. The bed is cool.

Note 2: lost word. This is the famous lost wax of Freemasonry. Fingered into shape in beeswax, the finished model is closely packed in plaster, sherds, brickdust. Then the whole is heated, and the wax runs out the channels or sprues left by its own melting. Molten metal is poured in and takes the wax's place. Later, when the metal is cooled, the mould is broken away, and the sprues or spurs of irrelevant metal hardened in the relief-channels are now broken off and filed down. The finished image, if all is well, now stands perfect to the first intention. The process is called *lost wax*. In some similar way, the creation of the physical world must have involved a Word spoken, a Word lost like wax, replaced by the dense matter of our own projection or illusion, more or less polished smooth.

CHAPTER V: QUINTESSENCE

It is the last hour of your life. Turn down the thermostat. Beyond Bhutan, exactly where you can't see it, is the cabinet of alchemic texts, the red telephone you can't use, the painful manuscript, the airconditioner plugged into the circuit too low in amperage to power it. The chemical lamp, all unseen things. The Brave Soldier has come at last to the bottom of the well. And finds himself in another house, just like all houses, every house. The wall. The wall might be the surface of what the Greeks, in nervous fear, ingratiatingly called the Hospitable, the Euxine Sea, a smiling most dangerous flatterer. We call it Black, and have forgotten to be afraid. The wall wants me to forget everything beyond its so casual opacity.

Courteous wall! Distinguish all! Discover the surface that evaporates off the sphere. Around the corner is the lintel, geometrical as Egypt, that cancels any further sight, and leaves us only Vision.

3

Something

It was something. The friends it had tried to persuade it it is nothing. It is. And although it is, it tries again and again to be less, even less. This was the first time, and thus it was about time. Later everything became itself more clearly, even simply, like a sign over the door reading women when you wanted one. So it was something but it did no good and things seldom ever did. This was how it goes, and this is it going. It was something and it was going, and that is something like anything is, and the way it was and the way it is, being it and only it, as if it were itself or had a self to be when that is only a way of speaking, and a casual way at that. Yet it was something and didn't seem casual to itself, although it couldn't tell itself what the difference was between what it thought it was being and what it seemed to be to anyone concerned with its seeming as by looking or reflecting back on some time when it was itself simply without question. So the question was and is more interesting than the thing it questioned the condition or nature of being by being. It was something, and it had friends. The question had friends too, so there looked to be no end to what they were likely to be doing around each other not being clear about anything more than the something it started out by imputing to the place it found itself in, as if to say, whatever this thing is I may be, it finds itself in a place, here, that is, to its measure, defined by my being there. This was not much and it is not clear even that it is enough. But it is something just as this is something, beyond question.

How the Day Begins

When we wake before dawn the first thing we have to do is unwind the massive brass clock Master bought in Varanasi until it relaxes enough to show us the ordinary time. Then we move from the sleeping apartments along the cloistered verandah to the necessary-house, where we relieve our bodies of that for which they have no further use. It is only then that we permit ourselves to step down into the tank, still at this season bathed with starlight (though to our all-too-ordinary eyes it appears more that the stars are bathing in the pool, proud Rigel—whom we call Kar-kang, on him the army of the sky stands firm against the assault of demon hosts and casual agnostic philosophies—stepping with us down into the tepid water).

We are laying our robes down on the water steps, we are entering the pool till the water reaches our waists. At the stroke of an arpeggiated tone on the iron harp, attendants (we do not see them now, for our eyes are studying carefully light ripple in the water's surface before each one of us) hurry by and whisk away our soiled robes. We hear someone clap his hands once, who?, and we step lower, till water spills into the little cup of our navels. Here and now begin to sing.

> Maker of Nothing and Nothing Made,
> Come without moving
> And without one shift
> Or stratagem
> We could call "attending"
> Attend to us,
> Hear without listening . . .

is the way the chant begins. During the last slokas of the last section, we begin to go deeper into the pond so that by the time of the Great Silence (counted by beats remembered, each of us silently keeping count inside, after all these years we're good at it and mostly do end our silences at once), the water has in effect made a fine bright loop or band around our bodies at the precise level of the heart. "Water, Bisector of the Heart's Fire," we begin chanting now, and now the order of the 'heartbeat' of the song moves quicker. Before the end of the verse, the water is at our throats and we stop going down, but do keep singing.

When that chant ends, the Vast Wordless begins, short as it is profound, we say of it, and we take the last steps till we stand on the very bottom of the tank, and the water is above the crown of the head of even the tallest of us, while the shortest of us already have some trouble holding their weight down in such a volume of water in the buoyant pond. It seems to me that the pond's bottom, stone slabs from the feel of it, slopes inward gently, so we can stand, each of us, at a suitable depth. Soon the Wordless is finished, and without ceremony of any kind we hurry out of the tank and find the clean robes that have been laid out for us, lying neat beneath towels, one for each of us, so that we have at this moment to share nothing but the water and the song.

Now it is time to pass through the one brass doorway into the low room where we take up our long-established positions in a half circle around the saffron-glowing screen of the monitor. We study what we see. Tiny rivers of electric current disturb the plasma closed in the glass and make it glow in lines we are are trained to find significant —numbers, letters, those special letters that are the seed of words. From this bright behavior we try to determine what has happened in the night of the world, or at least what has been happening that needs attention from us now, before the sun is permitted to rise.

Some of us have chosen (and we are permitted to do so) not to study the screen or make inferences from what is to be seen there, since it is thought by them unlikely that the past (the night, for instance, when it morning is) needs any other evidence of its effect but ourselves ourselves. We are consequences, some of us say, and everything we feel or think is consequence of everything that was.

Others of us say it is the very metaphoric ("likeness-having," we say) quality of the screen's 'evidence' that permits us to identify exactly what it is we feel, and relate it, even correlate it, with impending choice or undesirable futurities. And so armed, act.

Be all this as it may, this time is spent by us in scrutiny, whether of the shadows in our minds that are feelings themselves, or else the lightsome jerks of movement on the screen that, some of us think, connect with or describe those feelings best. We study during one Ordinary Period. About this time the sun is ready, and our troupe steps west with it towards the dining hall. We eat porridge with fruits (fresh in summer, dried now) cooked in it, and we drink tea. Some of us like milk in it, some of us butter, some of us salt, some of us sugar, but none all four. While the rest are eating and savoring the tea chosen for this hour, one of us reads aloud from the life stories of individuals so like ourselves that as we listen, our attention a little divided between eating and hearing, taste and comprehension, we sometimes almost justifiably imagine we are hearing about earlier passages in the life of our very selves.

Outside the large window, unglazed, no glass needed in it in our mild weathers, we see that a pale moon is setting, caught in the rays of the new day. Now some of us say it is sheer romance to pay attention whatsoever to the moon and what it's doing. "It does nothing, it is a rock in the sky. It's true that light stumbles over it from time to time, but that tells us nothing," they say. Others of us prefer to examine the course and colorations of this moon, arguing that for elegance of spectacle it can't be surpassed, especially in view of its moral innocence. It is just this innocence that yet others of us call into question—the moon is changeful. Changefulness, like all variety, is only too likely to encourage patience with cyclic existence, and thus impede our entrainment on the road to Illumination.

Still, the moon was setting, and we did watch it. Between it and the refectory window early birds were passing now and then, redfoot and wostle and waxwing, their hunting or warning cries blending into the even tenor of narrative as our reader gave us events in the Venerable Elder Prabhakirti's encounter with certain demons, who chose to appear in the form of large, many-storeyed houses in a crowded city far to the East. At first the Elder found himself trapped inside them, hurrying vainly from room to room by hallways and staircases that led nowhere, always empty, yet always full of noise—for us listeners, the shocking bray of the abbot's pet peacock eerily reinforced our understanding of the Elder's predicament. When the Venerable Elder at length became aware of the true, that is, energized-illusory, nature of his adversaries, he conjured them to unclose their rooms into the peaceful freedom of uttermost space. Which they presently did, leading the Venerable Elder out of the complicated buildings into the gardens, and there, between rows of young tomato plants, while an old-fashioned biplane chugged by overhead, the reformed demons undertook to abide by his directions. After the plane had passed down the sky, there was silence. Thereupon the Venerable Elder conjured this silence, and the great silence obeyed, and swore a binding oath that it would recur, and favor all the disciples of the Venerable Elder, and their disciples in turn, and so on, with calm in the midst of squabble, releasement in the middle of striving, and that this silence would be faithful from then onward, as long as this world-age lasted.

As the one of us who was reading came to the end of the assigned portion, we found ourselves granted a manifestation of that very silence. Marvelling at it, we sat for some time in joy. For such presences we lived. *Man for lucid absence born* we sang at the bottom of our morning meal, and seldom did we chant it with greater feeling, and even, it may be, with a sort of understanding. We washed our bowls out in quiet gratitude, then welcomed the first arrivers in the Audience Hall, to see what kind of work they had brought for us to do.

Sleepless Beauty

(a painting by Willem De Kooning)

The rush of pink—alizarin crimson denuded with white—
across the canvas! Sometimes a person looks so, a woman jumping back from the door when her angry hour coincides with the
long scheduled but completely forgotten visit from a man who
had once been a pretty good lover and who is now in the doorway plainly friendly and horny and holding a bunch of deep red
flowers and why doesn't she let him in and she's pissed off about
all kinds of things but not about him except that here he is when
she's completely forgotten ever inviting him, if she did, or agree-
ing to see him, and here he is and she's naked with just a scrap of
faded blue toweling around her not even hemmed. He should
have phoned.

All we see is what might be a woman and the fret of anxiety
that sends pretty sparks of color, marks, all around her, radiating
like the implications of a smart remark made at breakfast that
resound all through a pale morning—is it going to rain after all,
despite what the radio said? Despite what we see, there is only
what is not looking at us. Only the paint.

She was up all night. Night is one more white thing all
around us, it never matters, it never says anything. She has been
through all of it, trotting up Eighth Street after Mary's closed,
away from dawn, really, even though the light over the red
prison grew painfully intense as she hurried to the corner and
crossed the long way catercorner to the west side of Sixth where
Eve Sullivan was waiting to give her and everybody else a hard
time on their way down to Willie's. Why does she do it, go home
to Jersey. Why do I do it, go home to Bank Street and stay there,
no more drinking this week, no more going out, no matter who
calls.

And here is Ed, figuring to be given coffee or at least take her out for brunch, and then come back and screw her. He doesn't understand the changes in her. And as she realized that, how little he understood, she felt a tenderness for him and his ignorance, his greedy playful ignorance that kept humping at her; she resolved to let him make love to her.

But when the time came her eyes were burning and she held them closed, fighting off sleep, even though he felt good enough around and inside her, this little old puppy already with a baldspot between his ears. It was noon and she had been awake for twenty seven hours and he was puppying at her, puppydog tails, and bothering her with questions that were not phrased as questions, tricky ones like Long ago you always used to keep your eyes open I loved that I loved that.

Inside her everything was jumping out into the white. Everything is color but me, and everything is running away fast. No matter how much he puts into me I am always empty, paint drying in the sun that finally came out just after the latest eaters of lunch had walked down the steps of the Bamboo Village and gone back to work.

"Sleepless Beauty" is the sixth in a series called Imagines. The series examines and considers the consequences of certain lost or never-yet-painted pictures by celebrated painters.

Guanaco

–1–

There is an animal that lives where I have not traveled though a friend told me that when he was in that country he met an old wrestler I used to watch contend in my own suburb thirty-five years before and five thousand miles away. Up the hill from where they spoke over heavy bottles of imported but not very good beer, small round pellets of dung half hidden, already hard, gave some sort of evidence of such animals passing by night through the yellowed grasses of January.

–2–

Why do they move so deliberately? Why do they act as if we bore them no ill will, had no designs, didn't want meat, didn't want them to carry things around? Didn't want wool? Or is it wool? What is the difference, skin and skin, hair and hair?

–3–

Colors of like that. Teal blue that some see green. Electric blue that shocks the fingertips when realized in heavy rayon satin when. In the middle of the town a red bridge carries the main street over a remarkable cataract that no one stops to view, though it is legal to park, even on the bridge itself, and stand safely looking down at the mist arising from the crash of waters through the rocks, whitewater, spume of vapor from the mossy vault of the huge steel force-tube that stretches across the aprony downstream passage.

–4–

I don't know what I want. They all say that. And these hairy
creatures, supercilious as camels, know not much either. Arche-
ologists find their bones in association with human remains as
far back as the latter extend. Why are they waiting so long, what
for? I thought we were the only animals who kept waiting, are
kept waiting.

–5–

I picked the kind of t-shirt I wouldn't want to wear, and put
on uncomfortable shoes. Is this enough, I asked my looking
glass. No, it answered, there is still the matter of a hat, the
question of a bandana, the implication even you can't escape
making when you wear rowel spurs. Should I shave? You did. Is
there still time to water the plants? On the shoulders of Ararat a
queue of pilgrims saunters wearily up. Every ruin is its vocation,
and they can hear it call. Not every seeker has come home. Can I
leave yet? There is no door.

–6–

It's hard to find out whether people really like animals in
general, or the particular one you are studying. Mammals are
generally popular, though not the rat. Generally speaking, we
like what we can eat. Once on a mountain on the north of India I
looked at the red clay washed down the steep path by the mon-
soon. My footprint in the clay looked like anybody else's, if
larger. I stepped carefully, and a monk behind me smiled at me
when I looked over my shoulder; he said *Yeti, Yeti.* There was
nowhere I could go.

–7–

Is there a train that goes there? He thinks not. He got there
by climbing from rock to rock like a daffy shepherd in old
pastoral, wheezing (Gk: *asthma*) his love-songs and bruising his

small toe. The wisdom of those people did not record itself in
prose. For most of the climb he kept his necktie on, gift of his
mother, bearing a striped pattern in his family colors, unless he
got them wrong again. He stuffed it into his canteen case just
before the last meadow.

–8–

Things were tired there, or then. His analysis of their situation had bored them to inattention. They smoothed the barkless
white wood of their staffs with pebbles they'd cracked smartly
with heavy stones, to get a kind of flake or edge. He left the
reddish bark on his stick. Years later they still called him by that
name, or some word that meant what they had understood of all
he said: too much, too much indeed.

The New Fruit

It was the day in the long calendar when each person was allowed to design a new fruit. My turn was soon to come, and I was trying to turn my mind away from an alluring image of a cluster of soft blue elongated pods, like stubby plantains, fat fingers growing on a small hand. These were clearer in outer than in inner view; that fact alone, and that I had not built the fruit up from its innermost point (medicinal value) or its proximal inner (taste), had persuaded me that I had fallen for an obvious trope, in essence spray-painting a hand of bananas blue. No benefit in that.

Soon the flamens would be looking over their ivory scrollwork desktops at me, their eyes merely curious, their minds ready to binominalize, categorize and lexicalize the new fruit my mind would take from itself and offer, first time in the world, to them. Yet I, like each fructumittor, would suppose in that mere (I insist) limpid curiosity a certain element of amusement, disdain, even sarcasm, as if it fell to them to mock what it fell to others, on this one day of the long year, to propose. We live on a bridge over an unceasing river, dangerous the water, full of monsters and uncertain destinations.

Should it be blue at all? Blue had come first in my mind, tasteless in every sense, a blue fruit. This violation of the Color Code itself should have shown me that my thoughts were random and unformed. What was the matter with me today? *A fruit is its consequence, its taste, its texture, its capacity to dissemble the infancy of the seed, its rind, its heft to the hand of the planetary types who hold it, its color before the sun.* I knew the text as well as anyone, and yet I was within a few moments of

117

blurting out: let there be a blue fruit, its carpals swollen like sausages, its inner custardy and yum, with a taste to follow. What a gaffe! What a shame I would have been to my section. Yet someday a fruit could be designed, could it not, should it not, from the outside in?

But now the flamen addressed me: "Lucifer, what is your pleasure?" And I mumbled something small, reddish, roundish, no special taste, a bit mealy, the seeds will be protected over the coldest winter in Third Grade Planets, little seeds, pointy at one end, not too harmful if an animal swallows, a slight astringency in the flesh of the fruit, a slight caustic flavor to the rind, call it what you please.

Someday I will shape a lovely thing to suit myself, tint the light dark or taste the glitter alone of things, taste the inner pulp of color and know my blue fruit into the world.

Doctor of Silence

There is a man in our town who remembers Marius. In a plum waistcoat and heavy green serge knee britches, the celebrated leader would come to town every summer soon after Pentecost, and would spend a few weeks paddling in a pond and catching up with his paperwork. Sometimes in the evening he would settle down on the uncomfortable bench in front of the tavern and drink raw applejack with the locals. The man I'm talking about is old enough to remember how Marius had the peculiar trick of letting drops of the brandy linger on his upper lip without nervously flicking them with his tongue; this self-control was thought the sign of a superior person. When I was a little boy I used to practice keeping drops of milk or water on my lip, but I'd soon enough forget myself and lick away the tickle of their presence. Then I would go down to where the inn still stood, its linden trees absurdly fat now, and talk to the old man who remembered Marius. I would beg him again and again to tell about how Marius drank, or even, when I was bold, how Marius ate or walked or looked about him proudly while loosening the rough cambric kerchief he affected. But the old man would never say anything, never anything at all. This silence of his irritated me and the other young people; after a while though, it began to take on the quality of something admirable in itself, a trait of forbearance worthy of great Marius himself. Soon enough we thought better of ourselves and of our town for having such a learned, self-contained and sensible authority as a fellow-citizen.

Temple of Shiva

for Richard Marshall

"With a deep rose that seems even darker and thus less hectic" and the spirit had its own way with us, testing this small sentence-part against the broken circuits of its huge protective will. A deep rose, meant to say a color, said a flower, *un abîme*, as well, into which the lover fell, smooth as a glance into the shade on a sunny day. Listen, there are flowers that will suck the breath out of your lungs, flowers that blossom blue around the corner from your life, and lure you by fragrance alone to walk around there. In the shadow of the Shiva Temple, the cool "marble, the clean floors." I was surprised you found it so, marble, not the sensational obscurity of some icy Lingam secluded but much visited in an Himalayan cave. No, a rose. No, a rose so deep you have doubt of it. Listen, the priest reached up and shoved his ashy fingers so that they marked your forehead in Shiva's sign, the god we call dBang-Phyug, the wealthy, the lord of many cows. Old days in my life the ash came and touched me, on the day of it, Lent Spring, as if a smeary, greasy reminder. And the mind has oil, ash, anxiety, fingers of its own. Doctor Marianus answers your last prayer. The woman is home; she sits in your house. The trees remain outside, where they belong. If I can't persuade you, listen to the forest then. You heard it already, there, where the river had shrunk down to little more than a trickle, and you could, if I understood you correctly, step over it. Are we there yet? Is it still in her hands?

Domestic Symphony

(text beginning with a sentence of Martin Bookspan)

The applause of the Stuttgart audience continues for nearly five minutes. It tells how much all those hand-pair-owners (pity the poor monocheir) took pleasure in Strauss's *Sinfonia Domestica* just performed by the New York Philharmonic in Dresden's Liederhalle. Well might they be pleased. A house is for everyone, even a house that no one is allowed to enter except the Occupant and his entourage. Sans Souci, Nonsuch, the Winter Palace are for the likes of us, though we are not permitted to enter, never were allowed in, we trash. And you can't come into my house either, all you Sforzas and Plantagenets. Each being stands inside his noblest shell and reigns and reigns and smiles out at the fall of evening shade—this is the hour of mastery. The Baby shrieks in his nursery, the Wife exults in the late peace of the Husband's exhausted quiet. Stillness and sunset. The hood of the Mercedes is still tepid in the breezeway, the radio is softly reminding everybody that violins get on nobody's nerves, that melody was the Devil's answer to sickness and death—sustain, o great smooth oozing song the upswelling intervals this fine old Bavarian discovered to know me with, sevenths and ninths and even wider outrage. A house belongs to everyone who hears the word "house" or "haus" or "oikia" or "khang.ba." We walk in through the sound and exult at the rich furnishings, how they are spread through a sense of space so proliferated in every direction that there is no end of our being at home. The baby can bell and the nurse can scold and the cat can fiddle and the spoon run away with the wife, and all will be well in such a place, because we are at home. And music like this puts us at our ease, bends the necessitous clamor of our hearts (for we are all heroes) to accommodate the *sense of adventure* without in fact leaving the urgent comforts of this caravanly house, this earthly indoor paradise. That is why they are applauding, that their small crowded apartments are full of crocheted tablecloths covering oaken tables with walnut shells stuck in the loops of the cloth from last night's dinner still, that the copy of Gorky's autobiography is still open on the edge of the bathtub waiting for your soak this quiet midnight, that though you've been reading it for more than a week it has still not fallen into the water, as you dread enough to worry about it during the duller passages, but not enough to suspend this fairly irresponsible way of reading what is, on the other hand and after all, your own book. You are applauding because there is still some bacon left in the icebox and the girl you tried to get to go with you to The Green Lion knew better and refused, pleading her aunt's ill health. You are applauding because after the concert there is nothing you have to do except walk slowly through the safe streets of your native city to your own crowded, intimate, interesting apartment. You don't have to pray, talk to anyone, write a word, turn a handle. You are applauding because you are alone, and music, since it is always in the past (basic rule of physics, velocity of sound, and so forth and so on) by the time you hear it, music is always alone, can only be apprehended alone. You are alone, and safe, and owe nothing to anyone at all, except to the State. And the State at this hour is surely asleep.

Dog

In a former life this grey dog who now sits up behind the wheel of a blue late-model Plymouth, wearing a red webstrap leash and responding through the closed window to the affectionate blandishments of pedestrians affectionately, was a minister of a remote parish in the western hills of Massachusetts. In this life it is a cute dog, a *cute* dog as I hear them stress, long hooting ooo of their voices, as they leave off tapping on the car window and walk smiling away. But in that life the Rev. Issachar Weekes was, while presentable enough, hardly cute, not enough so, at any rate, to attract unblushing endearments from respectable women, even on Sunday evenings, even in that society so notoriously clericophilous.

Listening, as I often do, to the ceaseless chit-chat at the back of my mind (I call it the Akashic Record when I seek to impress new acquaintances), I learn that the Rev. Mr Weekes once banished a great mangy sheepdog from the church on a nasty winter evening, right in the middle of vespers. The poor dog had mooched in at the heels of an arthritic woman slow to get the big oaken door closed, and had huddled up shivering beside the pulpit to find some little warmth. Thence he had been dislodged by the priestly Weekes, who prodded the beast along with his boot, right out into the snarling wind and snow.

The Lords of Karma, at watch even in Episcopal jurisdictions, took careful note. The rustic congregation itself was disheartened by their priest's unwonted lack of compassion, especially since he had turfed the dog only seconds after intoning, with the worshippers, *He hath put down the mighty from their seat, and hath exalted the humble and meek.*

123

The dog was not seen again in the parish, and the natural speculation was that it had expired in the night. No remains were discovered, however, and Opinion had meatier provender than missing dogs, so the affair rested. Some old folks tended to remember that exceptionally severe winter as The Year Parson Booted the Dog, but soon enough they too had other things to think about, what with Napoleon raging in Europe and the British bothering our midlands. Long winters brought short harvests, and nobody could blame the parson for that.

The Lords of Karma, however, those scrupulous transpersonal magistrates who care as much about a Weekes as they do about Napoleon, or an old dog, for that matter, jotted the event down in its proper place. And after the soul that had been Weekes tried several times to incarnate once more as a human being (a condition to which the general probity and earnestness of its recent Weekes life entitled it), only to find itself stillborn or dead in infancy, the Weekes-soul appeared as a suppliant before the Karmic Court, seeking a remedy. The judges reminded him of the incident of the dog.

The Weekes remembered it only after some effort, and recalled with it a season of poor digestion, a time marked by a thoroughly unsatisfactory correspondence with his diocesan dean—these were offered as extenuating circumstances. The judges agreed that Weekes had been vexed severely, yet they gently insisted on the ineluctable character of the karmic process. Weekes had to become a dog before he could become man or woman again. He might choose to become a lap-dog (though these were becoming unfashionable in recent decades), a dog doted on by its master, or even a cute dog in a blue car, but a dog of some sort he had to be.

So it is that a friend today, herself not very fond of dogs, tapped like all the rest at the car window and amused the dog. Its friendly unintelligent eyes gave no clue to its soul's next port of call. Perhaps only a banker or a bishop. Or maybe this beribboned poodle will one day come to life as a great man, theoretician of an as yet undreamt-of science; he might be the ultimate commentator on Dante, or the destined discoverer of Lazarus's lost gospel. Maybe the dog made some contact with me (I saw it first, I too smiled at it through the window), and will choose to be born in some year to come as my own little son, and I will see him all the days of my life playing among my books and records beneath the images on my wall of the unalterable deities, Jampal who cuts through the rationalizations of the mind, and Chenre-zi, who bends low to hear the whimper of every living thing.

The Man Who Read
Meister Eckhardt

It was not a matter of knowing God. He had learned it was a matter of knowing *in* God. Being in divine knowledge. He had studied. He knew the words people said, especially the great ones, Eckhardt, Tauler, Merswin, Suso. He knew the way, sometimes, between one page and the next, his eyes would go out of focus, yet his knowingness would be filled. Before he could really know what he was knowing, the unread page would flicker into view. He would sigh and go on reading and not knowing.

One evening, after a tiring day, he sat in a small recital hall listening to a trio sonata of Bach. The program notes, which he read carefully, explained that the work had begun life as an organ sonata, and had only recently been transcribed by the group's violinist into the simple, perhaps even simplistic, event he was hearing now.

Methodically, instrument gave way to instrument, the modest material passed back and forth, as if sons were examining the dubious bequest of their dead father. He wondered what it would be like to hear music as God hears it.

No sooner had he thought that than he stopped thinking anything. Without time to admit he might be making a large misstep, he found himself overwhelmed with knowing, and he welcomed it. Violin and piano and cello, still perfectly audible, shared his mind with a fierce reedy old organ that stormed and guided behind the present instruments like a mother lioness sorting out her cubs. As soon as he sensed that, the animals of his metaphor began to rampage across an apt, unending veldt. Outside, though, an icicle was dripping tunefully above the church door in the gaunt Leipzig street. A block away an old

126

woman pressed the varicose veins that threaded her calves. The organ grew louder (though the modern instruments remained perfectly distinct), and the voices of the score began to peel off and represent themselves in other timbres and other sonorities, those he could name and those he had never heard.

These soundings of theme and re-entrance now turned upside-down, turned mirror-inverted, retrograde-inverted, inside out, completely independent of what Bach meant them to do at any given moment. Spurs of music vertically soared or mined down into the earth below which the stately horizontal tread of the three dull instruments continued.

But he, the knower, could not shelter in chaos or blur, despite all the clash of contradictory directions and passing dissonances—the lines of the music itself, *this* music, remained ever too clear. So did the town harlot in Cöthen, bundling her breasts warm with old newspapers. So did a Swedish army hurrying across a frozen lake into Courland. So did a Victorian music master analyzing this very sonata with languid blonde children in a brownish house. So did a tree on an Italian hillside, bare of fruit, scarred where a duelist's wild shot had grazed the bark in the tree's youth and set up a ripple of distortion still represented years later accurately in the growing wood. This wood, still alive and leafy growing, was also the sonorous substance from which this cello later would be, had been, made. He could see the maker, hear the râles of his last illness, hear money chinking down in Milano, Zurich, Mannheim. He followed the wood chips and sawdust into the fires where North Italian children celebrated Epiphany; cookies cloying with anise crumbled from their mouths and were eaten by ants in the furtive night. He watched the ants, and followed them to all their nests, and observed their behavior in their immense cities. Fear began to overwhelm him.

He saw everything, and nothing stayed. Each thing he tried to bless as it passed, the fearful with the sad and the ominous, every blessed thing, god or godly as he was in this fugue of knowing. He saw the ancestors of these musicians struggling through Europe, taking ship in Trabzon and Odessa and Constanta, coming and going and conceiving offspring with an unbelievable casualness, calm ignorance of the consequence that he, now, was bearing for all of them.

As he sat forward to ease the congestion of images that crowded his awareness, he knew, as in the perfect calm of the whirlwind's abnegating core, that one can risk knowing *in* God only in the safety of silence, in the inner chamber, eyes closed, where there are no works of humankind to expand in all their incalculable immensity. Even a word never ends. All the reading he had done came close to preparing him for the enormous separation he was beginning now to traverse. He knew he was being lost into the rich intricacy of what was, though he could never see it as, design.

As he sat forward, a voice (tempter or redeemer he could not guess) spoke gently in him: This is why Eden. This is why that tree of knowledge, that ominous taste, to limit human knowledge to what can be known in separation. You men are masters only in isolation. You are princely separates. Your strength lies in not seeing the consequences, not noticing the adamantine latticework that holds each thing (real or imagined or imputed) rigorously in place. This network is my music. Come hear in me.

By the mercy of gravity, his tensed body, now slack, remained in its seat, in no way disturbing the recital. Only when the players concluded, smug with a unison that came almost by surprise, and the audience was applauding cordially, did the body succumb to vibration and slip into the dark quiet trough between the rows of seats tenanted for a time by people just like him.

Dracaena

for John Yau

–1–

It is a mistake to expect a snake to be rational. The leaves of the new dracaena on the table under the window fan are long and striped with white, so that in section a leaf might resemble the tricolor of Nigeria, is it, green white green.

–2–

In Africa, it follows, there are many serpents. He said that one morning as he walked to the mailbox he looked down and saw there must have been thirty of them. He was listening to Liszt's *Etudes for Transcendental Execution,* important that things have their truest names, not that any truly are, that we can say. He said they come down the mountain, or down from the mountain.

–3–

Of course that isn't Africa and never was. It is the very ancient peneplane so deeply eroded that it looks like mountains now. The snakes are more recent, and it is important never to kill one.

–4–

Tibetans have a saying: Lang tong, ta ja, dül chik.
The leaves of the dracaena, while I haven't studied them

with any care, remind me of snakes, and their name is snaky too, like the Latin draco from which our word dragon comes, but which means snake.

–5–

Liszt has a tone poem called in French by words that mean: That which is heard on the Mountain. They come down. I have always loved mountains, and the feel that comes over my mind, like a cool morning fog the eye can penetrate far enough for all its purposes, and know a valley well peopled beyond. The feel of being on a morning mountain. But what about these snakes, what do they do to my feeling? And what do they feel?

–6–

Killing one snake releases as much anger as killing a hundred horses, a thousand cows, is what the Tibetans mean.

What about killing a flower, did you ever? But this thing doesn't blossom, does it? I never saw it, and just for once I don't want a flower that grows only in a book.

–7–

At the door to my friend's hermitage a small ordinary garter snake has its dwelling, and is to be seen on sunny days trying to keep out of sight under the foliage while still keeping some in some rays. Every now and again another serpent comes, this one silver and burgundy in color, no bigger, milk snake. All this is rational and describable. But what about our fear?

What about our feelings?

–8–

The women looked up and found that a large snake had crept into the doorway. One of them lifted her long skirts and took a flying leap over it and out into the yard. The snake looking up thought: These people are even more remarkable than I supposed; not only can they walk, they can fly. I will stay near them and learn to know their minds, and so one day perhaps my own.

–9–

My friend from Bengal, her mother would never say shap, the word for snake, but always say only lota, lota the Creeper. If you talk its name, it comes. Once one had played with her ankles and she didn't like it. Nor would I. By now the Lazar Berman recording had ended, and there was no more music. The tape had coiled back into its cassette and rested.

–10–

Whenever I am in a house with many indoor plants, I think of Brahms. This is especially true with palms, aloes, and dracaenas, less so with ordinary vascular plants through whose veins invisibly alchemic essences despised by Marxist analysis still consent to flow.

Thinking of his mountain, a little house from which all else can be seen, I put on the B flat Sextet. Already it seems like morning.

4

Hair

Can it be spoken or written

a city of old stones

there are shadows
intolerable heat from glary sky
shadow is always explaining something

the trifles that are alphabets
twigs of course
                    or how
a dry leaf sits on a rock

and of what bright preoccupation
is what we call human intelligence the shadow?

she wrote. The people who lived in this city were interested in
this problem. Then one day they heard a scream falling from the
sky, and all bets were off.

–2–

There were a few cars parked nearby. From one of them a
girl climbed out and walked towards the largest pile of ruins. She
wore shorts that had been white, and a yellow t-shirt. She was of
a Red Dakini nature, her ample hair loose and uncontrolled in

135

the hot breeze, the flesh round her slim thighs the only hint of inseverity in this whole terrain. It was painful to watch her, and remember, and wonder what had brought us in our separate lives, whoever she is, to this painful, yes, it was a painful place.

It was her hair that drew me back, dry as it was, because it was wild. Wildness has quickness in it, lacking here in the sluggish brutality of the weather. To follow her I had to cross the trashed central plaza, stepping past lizards on their grey-green weeds, one of them sporting a tiny white flower over which three bees squabbled.

I have told it before. There is nothing to say again. We are in love with babies because nothing has ever happened to them. We celebrate the success of their forgetfulness. On their pudgy smoothness we can project our unexamined hopes. We are in love with ruins because they show us something worse than even our present condition, sordid as it is. Ruins promise a a subtle relaxation from our daily striving—don't worry, it all amounts precisely to this. How hard we all have to work to be where we are. Between the soulless baby and the the workless ruins, our placid hopeful whining souls shuttle back and forth, avoiding the moment.

–3–

She is there, in what had been a room once, bedroom, machine shop, private chapel, dentist's office—all function sublimed away in the pure quadernity of blank structure. Shadowy and hot in here, and she moved in the shadows listlessly, evidently pursuing something with the same lack of conviction with which I followed her now.

–4–

By a stretch of the word I could say we were there together: she was there and I was there and nobody else was. The people who came in those other cars—no sign of them. What brings them here? Some hope of knowing, of picking up a stray fact or knack from the ruin of what once made sense, or sense enough to make a building stand and a city full of people? They nose around the ruins, seeking, measuring, consulting scraps of paper in their hands, pacing out directions and distances, their eyes on the moon disk or the first rays of the morning sun, their feet scuffing along over brick and plaster and scraps of aluminum. Do they find what they seek?

When I did come out, hours later, hers was the only other car left. Even the maroon and mustard sedan of the military police was gone. I will say it then: we were together in the ruined city.

I can say it. I can write it, here, in my mother tongue, and see what happens. It will go from ink to ink, language to language. *Insieme* they will say, and *len-chik*, but will it be true? Will my translators make it true?

She was here, with me, with her wild dry hair, her imaginable thighs, her tensions that kept her moving before me deeper into the once-used spaces. She was very young.

–5–

A dog is barking now and a dog was barking then. I was nowhere but together, hot. I have some fear of dogs. Less now than when I was younger, but still there. Still fear. The dog that was barking then seemed far, and its odd slow belling drew no nearer. Lizards was it chasing? Or diving up madly at the sulfurs and mauve papilios that marked the tattered springtimes in this sere region?

–6–

It was comfortable enough to trail behind her through the ruins. No one had made them into a museum. They were what they had become, and the only attentions we afterlings had favored the place with were prime looting and tardy pilfering, tiny mingy vandalisms almost benign, almost sweet (because personal) in the general wreckage Time had made of things. I picked my way through the evidence, mostly interested in it, I can be interested in anything. I'm never bored, God, no. That's the least of my problems. I followed her mostly because she was there, because she was moving, because she was young, because she was woman. I had a lot of training in following women. It was comfortable. She set up a current I elected to drift along.

–7–

The part of the city we negotiated now (still this fictive "we"—but allow me the dim sensuous pretense of this mingler, this connubial pronoun) had been once a complex with very large separate buildings. In their fall, the groundplans had grown thought-provokingly mixed. Room led to room, rooms (all of them once modular, prefabricated perhaps) were now embedded in other rooms, and a helter-skelter of floors at every stable angle made horizontal progress often a vertical ploy. There was climbing to be done, and sliding, as we, casual verb coming with casual pronoun, strolled apart together through the ruins of our ancestral city.

–8–

What could this suite of rooms have been? Chinese Embassy? Dealer in curios? Malaysian restaurant? Salon of a connoisseur? Ballroom of a theme hotel? Red walls, smashed bronzes, decapitated ceramic arhats were there, and we were there with them. Should I describe us? A young woman bent to study the head of a bodhisattva still upright in the corner. A man watching her.

–9–

She wouldn't talk, I wouldn't make love. Apart from that, we got along pretty well when we finally caught up with each other, when she, then I, stumbled out of one dark room into another, and found the dark different, ruddier, hotter, and knew we were outdoors, on a blasted piazza soon after sunset, hedged in on all sides by what had fallen.

–10–

I'm fond of outdoors, even this one, which seemed even hotter now that the visible occasion of heat had disappeared in a red ruin of its own. Without discussing it we fell into step and walked, or clambered, side by side back in the direction we guessed would take us to the parking lot. When we got there and found ours the only ones left, we sat down cross-legged on the warm earth halfway between hers and mine.

I talked and she listened alertly, so alertly in fact that I wondered if she understood my language at all well, or if I was making any sense. It had been a long while since I'd had anything to say to anyone, and maybe I'd forgotten the knack of it. Still, talk is safe enough, whatever they may say. And I talked on, about my reactions to the ruins, my plans for the days ahead, and even more generally, about the shabby guesswork that serves me for a Philosophy of Life, the arrogant dreaminess that serves for my theology. From time to time she spoke.

–11–

Words in my language, natively pronounced, with an oceanic accent. New Zealand maybe. Not many of them, just enough to keep me going. Going is talking. As I think they were meant to, keep me going, an easy job, she could have used fewer. It was important for me to talk as long as possible, to stave off the moment we would have to decide what to do with each other, with the night, with our cars, with this landscape it would be good to abandon, together.

–12–

We were bonded somehow, that was clear. My padding along in step behind her so long had seen to that: a rhythmic link had been established. Bonded, linked, connected. Now I was all too well aware that people, me least of all, can't just rest content with an awareness of being connected with somebody else. We all have to do something about it. Usually what we do in the name of the bond breaks the bond. "I feel such a deep connection with you!" are the first words of a long song (and dance) that ends with "good-bye." Or am I wrong. You tell me.

–13–

In the old days when I worked for a living, some odd day would come when I'd pass through the door into the office and no one would be there. The men's room door would be locked, the clock stopped. It would seem that everyone else had decided, or been directed, to take a holiday, or that some unharbingered economic catastrophe had caused everybody to flee across the nearby border. Everybody but me. I'd sit there smoking and feeling, delighting in the sudden spaciousness of time, delighting in change for its own sake. What is more delicious than difference?

Yet I was uneasy too (less than another might be—I am a calm man); here were a spaciousness and a freedom I couldn't really use because I didn't understand. And because I didn't, I didn't know if it would last. I'd spend that magical quarter-hour worrying about whether it would last. Then the doors would fly open and workers come hurrying in struggling out of their coats and blaming buses and alarm clocks. One by one each would contribute to the sordid (because ordinary) history of what had led to such an extraordinary state of affairs. We'd all get down to work, and time would have its way with me again.

–14–

We were bonded, and I didn't want to do anything about it at all. Obviously the demons who arrange such matters meant us to seduce each other, for the sheer lack of anything better to do, seduce and carry one another off to some problematic rendezvous just over the horizon. There we would enjoy one another, explore one another, please one another, exploit one another, bore one another, till each of us was ready for the next complication in our separate meaningless destinies. No thanks. It hurts too much. Her, if not me. She is tender and intelligent and sensuous, I thought, and so am I. I don't want to hurt her, she doesn't want to hurt me. Let the bond take care of itself, thought I. If it's a real bond, it's adequate. If not, why pretend. A bond is adequate.

−15−

It isn't that we chose each other. Still, we were chosen. I could look at her and imagine a sort of ocean that would give me, entering it, a lot of comfort in this parched wilderness. I once got from a friend in southern France a hologram postcard of a tanned naked woman leading a white saddled horse up out of the blue Mediterranean. She calls past the horse's head to a friend, or else her mouth just hangs open in sun glare. Gasping at the flare. Red white and blue, the tricolor I suppose the covert point is. My mind wanders, my will wavers. I look at her. She is wondering why I've stopped talking.

−16−

I was talking again and the breathy mythy oceanic moment passed. We sat on the hot dry ground like old friends and it got dark. "Real dark," she called it, and her phrase scared me, as if it meant something more final than night. I stood up and touched for the first time the fine wild dry tangle of her dirty hair.

−17−

It isn't that I abhor risk. I wouldn't have been there, none of us would be here, without some taste for jeopardy—the game divided against itself, the subtle bondage of everyday circumstance, the subtle slavedrivers that other people are to us. It was a sure thing I was avoiding: desire leads to grief by loss. Better take a short cut and have the loss direct, without all the flurry and explanations and hopes. False hopes. So my point in standing up had been to say good-bye. The point blurred when she stood up too, in that one movement both confirming my gesture and subtly annihilating it. For we were at par again, peers, both on our feet, with everything still to be done.

–18–

Why had I touched her hair? I had given way to desire, that's why. I admired this hair. It was sexy—out of control, wild, abundant, exuberant, profligate. It was dry, matching the terrain. It made her seem less like a person and more like a telluric figure—I was smitten with exaggeration. I wanted to touch this hair, this talismanic supernatural mop of over-measured tawniness, this mane. I wanted to touch it, and I touched it. It felt like hair. Felt just as I expected it to feel. I knew that the touch would haunt my hand a while, minutes or hours. I knew that later, when I was sleeping alone, I'd feel the feel in my hands and regret, maybe bitterly, not going with her. That pain would serve me right, for touching.

–19–

And she, whose hair was touched, what would she feel? Would she have regrets? That's for her to know, and for me not to conjecture about, not at all. She's alive, she can feel for herself, do what she wants, as much as any of us can. Which is not much, but enough. What did I want to do?

–20–

Want is a curious word. Means 'lack.' What do I lack, what do I need, or need done? What I lacked, from one point of view, was someone to travel with, someone to behave to and perform for and complain to or blame. Someone to love, in other words. I wanted to love a lot of people. Everybody can use some love. Why with her? I didn't want the grief.

–21–

These were my disheveled reflections and I smiled at her, said my good night and began walking to my car, parked in deep shadow by the base of a ruined monument on which two legs stood, male, broken off mid-thigh, against the starry sky. Why

had I said good night and not good-bye? The angry sun was gone
and the moon was rising, gibbous, a moon fit for ruins. Good Bye
means (I read this somewhere) "God be with ye"—an acceptable
sentiment, though hardly supported by what passes for my theology. The meaning, if it has a meaning, is at least projective,
companionable. But I had said good night. And she asked, using
more words right now in sequence than she had so far used
altogether, where was I staying and where was I headed and
would we meet in the morning.

–22–

Few people know me, and of the ones who do, few talk to
me about myself. Those who do unite in declaring me a polite
man, at least in speech. Polite to a fault, some have added. I
don't care one way or another. If I am so polite, it's not something consciously applied. I suppose I was reared well, hence my
politeness doesn't mean much, not personally. Then again, politeness isn't supposed to be conscious or mean much—just to
be a reflex of and in good society, as consoling and empty as a
warm breeze.

This politeness of mine arrested me now and made me try
to answer her. Think of an answer. I tried to think of where I'd
stay, in the car I guess, but that sounded so forlorn, a sad plea for
company. I didn't feel sadness—it's just built into the words.
How could I explain to her that I had no idea where I was
headed? Where the road goes. That sounds pompous as I am,
more romantic than I dare concede.

So I walked back in the dark and put my arms around her.
That was the quietest thing to do.

–23–

Pressing her lean warm body to mine I realized two other
things simultaneously: that this embrace was not exactly what
she had had in mind, and also that it was not unwelcome to her.
She smelled of sweat, recent sweat, not repellent, as I was sure I
did too. She yawned, and lay her head on my shoulder, while I

busied my face in her fascinating hair, here at last to some degree possessed. We stood that way until it seemed unnatural to go on standing.

–24–

And so one thing, as usual, led to another. Naive of me (I am naive) to think there could ever be an exception. The moment I noticed her hair, hours before, across the plaza, and chose (did I choose? of course I chose) to follow her, and it, through the ruins, our fate was sealed. As they say. Not a horrible fate, just one more complexity, one more knot in the gnarled fiber of our terrible history. Let it pass. The pain, there will have to be pain, will pass too. Let it pass.

–25–

My car was small, full of the plausible junk I have never been able to resist acquiring and keeping by me. Emergency alternatives, enough for a second life. Why list them? Imagine them, we all have plenty. Stuff it in a small Korean car and you have the picture. That's how it was. So we went to her car, bigger and empty, curiously empty. She rolled the seats down and rolled the windows up quickly against the already attentive mosquitoes. We got out of our clothes as we lay into the big car's moulded cushions. I was rehearsing in mind exactly how I was going to explain that I didn't want to make love, how to say that without seeming to reject her, or seeming more of a simpleton than I had to. How to be clear. Midway in this silent analysis, I found we were already making love, just as I was reaffirming my fresh decision not to do this very thing we were convincingly doing.

–26–

Apparitions haunted us all night. Whatever we had done to each other by making love (I must someday stop and examine that expression, "making" love) or by doing it in that place, the energies in our surround were all stirred up. During the fitful hours we slept, covered with each other's sweat, the dark outside the car would break with vagrant pallors, shifting uneasy colors, shapes unpleasantly incomplete. I for one felt disturbed, almost nauseated, by these phantoms, but not at all menaced by them. Of course I wanted to slip out of the car, hurry to my own and be gone before she woke. Already I was deploring our liaison, but there it is, the "our" again, dreary offspring of the "we" who wandered so blithely through the ruins and through my earlier daytime syntax. It was our thing already, and I wanted no part of it.

Why didn't I just get out and go? As well might a suicide plummeting from a romantic bridge ask himself: Why don't I just stop falling? Things entrain us. Long sentences uncoil from the effortless machine, and we are spoken to the bitter or the boring end.

Did I feel any tenderness for her? Considerable. Was I full of post-coital revulsion? I was not. She was lovely, and her wet body slithering in sleep against mine as we tossed was a joy to me. I was not strictly enjoying myself. Ominously, I was enjoying what there was of us.

–27–

I imagined that the apparitions that bothered us were not ghosts of this city's sudden myriad dead. Recent as their catastrophe was, I supposed the ghosts were already gone, busy in the Bardo ripening rebirths, or slanging in hell, or whatever, as they say, does ensue. These phantasms were either demons and angels made visible by the extreme complexity of the energy-field at this point on the earth's surface (catastrophes charge their regions), or else perturbations of this already supercharged turbulence by emotional energies imprudently set free as we made love.

–28–

Chaste I had hoped to cross the deserts, chaste to come to the new settlements rumored in the east. To get there without old encumbrance, old flexes of desire. Men, like cultures, discover an attractiveness in chastity only at moments of extreme stress. It is stupid to go on and on about this. People can be chaste together, sex can be chaste. But that isn't what I *mean*, whines the poor little word. Chastity. A white sky, a blue sky. What difference does it make among all the ruins?

–29–

Before morning my ragged sleep turned full. I went deep under, and woke stifled, scorched and alone. The sun seemed almost at noon. I was vigilant with discomfort. I climbed out into the more spacious suffocation of the plaza. No cloud. In the small shadow of the car itself, made larger by the trunk roof raised like a canopy, she crouched over food and soluble coffee. She gave me some, and I saw that the trunk of her car was full of foodstuffs, neat as a pantry.

I needed to make water more than I needed to drink, and did so, beyond the monument and on its base, modestly. As late as it seemed, the plaza was empty. No tourists or travelers today. The heat seemed already worse than yesterday's, and I began to long for the hills I could see perfectly well off east of the ruins, haze over them, and a guess about mountains beyond.

–30–

It's not that I have to be sure about it, not at all. I could tell only about the taste of what is offered, the high abrasive thinness of the instant coffee and the very sweet rolls she took out of a can. Or I could tell about the rainstorm in which we made shift both to dance and shower, baby naked. We even managed to get cold—but that was later, in those successful hills. I liked traveling in two cars, illusion of independence. Wasteful, I suppose, but waste is our only luxury now. And the power cells were fully charged, we could go for a long time. We drove, each in own car, tailing or leading each other, convoy of two, no talking, no talking, only able to guess at the other's intentions. Always the exciting notion that at any point she might stop and I keep going, irretrievable, far. Or she could. No vice without its versa.

–31–

People came to see the ruins really just to see what it had been like. Most of them could remember it anyway, or something just like it, why bother. Why did I bother? You couldn't see what it had been like, only what it is now, jumbled and complex, after. What was the sense of it, now, after. They had been pretty much all alike, anywhere, and their ruins even more so. The things that had been different—colors, languages, currencies, flags—were gone now. Paper money and the other gods. Gone. All rubble speaks the same language, the same florid rhetoric of ruin. There were little dialect differences (stone, concrete, alloys of steel), but what difference does difference make?

Why had I come? If I asked myself (I asked myself), the answer would come (did come): to find her. Does this mean a comforting readjustment of expectation to match accomplishment? Maybe. Does it mean anything, this answer rising so clearly in my thought as if it were implicit in the question? As if one asked any question at all merely as a logical preamble to blurting out the answer, the clear, the irreducible *This is the case* that burns to be spoken?

–32–

I don't know much about dogs, and don't much like them, though I once had companionable relations with a blue Australian sheepdog. I've never had a dog, if that's the verb, and they generally, well- or ill-behaved, make me uneasy. Especially nowadays, so many wild. Sometime I'll have to tell about the doubts I have about people who have dogs. They have dogs, I have doubts—maybe even for the same reason. Doubts make good company.

But about dogs. In the old days they used to have many kinds of dog food—I can remember cheese-flavor, beef-flavor, liver-flavor, hamburger-flavor, milk-flavor and mixed. No doubt there were many others, it's not important, but these are the ones I remember. Some of them were shaped like bones, others were kibbled, result of an operation I have never understood. The word is interesting. But what I am trundling so awkwardly towards is this: what made a given dog prefer one of these flavor types to all the others? There were dry foods and moist foods, and surely semi-dry and semi-moist, but forget texture for a moment. Why did Dog A (we'll call it that, just to be clear in the few cases—all of them hypothetical, alas—where we can be clear) (we?) choose, out of all the bowls arrayed (we generously imagine) in front of it, the one (say, cheese-flavor) to which it would return whenever it got a chance, comfortedly, day after day? In case I've grown too abstract (is that the word?), let me say clearly that I'm talking about choice. The mystery of preference. Why does a tabula rasa-type dog, a dog we'll suppose never having tasted anything except bitch-milk, opt for the one special sort of food? If dogs do.

I see I have involved myself in many imponderables. I don't know enough about dogs to make sense of this imaginary dog ("A") we are watching wolfing down some of the (no longer available) choicefully chosen dog food. It's all gone, all gone. There are still dogs aplenty, and I don't know much about them. What do the poor things eat now? They eat what they can find. But our nice imaginary dog, and its selected food, why, why? What is the mystery of choice? Why do we choose what we choose? What do we choose when we choose? Our earliest Buddhist poet ponders the question deeply, and devotes to it a whole act of *A Midsummer's Night Dream*, a play I remember fondly. I should re-read it, I should get a book. My memory tells me that his young lovers, falling in and out of love as their perceptual systems (he says "eyes") are influenced by a roguish sprite's herbal lotions, consistently talk about love as appetite, and their various beloveds as favored foods. We know what it means to be hungry. Is there such a thing as affinity, link, bonding? Is there such a thing, such a case, as choosing? What is choice? What

makes us choose? How is what is chosen chosen? Stray dogs
that we were, we came there to choose each other.

—33—

But we came, we thought, to see the ruins. To see how we
lived then. A "we" that is more like "they," we were them then,
and now we're only who we are. If that.

What I'd seen as I wandered through the ruins confused me.
The memories I had were already confused with the memories I
ought to have. Almost everybody remembers the assassinations
of Caesar, Lincoln, Kennedy. History is synthetic memory im-
plant, smooth mnemonoids slipped in, personal and social
memories inextricable, each one of us was Herod writhing in the
arena in his silver shirt.

And my memories, actual and synthetic identical by virtue
of appearing undifferentiably on the identical stage, the mind,
were convulsed by the simple unlikeliness of rubble. Nothing
was more likely than I, than a woman with ample dry hair, wild.
A thin woman who gave me food.

—34—

Now we were going into the eastern mountains. It was
warm again after the rain we'd found in the foothills, but nothing like the wicked heat on the plain of ruins. Down there it was
clear that demons, who, under civilized urban conditions recede
into the inner texture of daily life and work their small indecen-
cies inside machines, routines, projects of real estate developers
and reformers, inside computers and amplifiers and calendars,
had now after the collapse of mechanized distraction returned to
their native landscapes, and dwelled again in rock and cave and
weather. Demons too are pastoral sentimentalists. Demons too
once lived in Arcadia.

So the demons present where we traveled were mountain
devils, an austere, cruel lot, to be sure, but not given to toying
with their victims. Not for them the mirage, the *fata morgana*,
the dizzying heat stroke, the gradual dehydration of flesh and

wit. These wielded gruffer troll-tools, avalanches and blizzards and washed-out roads. They broke bridges rather than hearts, and were too fierce to slay lingeringly.

But they did nothing to us, unless leaving us alone to our own intimate journeyings was sadism enough. Maybe the sour sweat of the lowlands was still on us, maybe the wound of our budding relationship was torment enough to gratify them. It is well known that demons leave lovers alone in the first weeks of relationships, since lovers do demon work gladly on each other, gladly, and call it caring, daring, sharing. Things like that.

−35−

Lovers. The words that just slip out. In the cave. In the car. Piecemeal words, piecemeal lives. We were getting there. Her hair.

What did I care about my life, the things I had planned. I had planned nothing. I only plan things to avoid. Nothing makes sense before it's there. Here. How could I know what I was feeling? Feeling is not knowing. Like two of the great sacred rivers (Ganges and Brahmaputra? Sutlej and Indus?) they rise in the same mountain watershed, flow through different religions and water different hopes, then fall into the same endless sea. Same? But to move along one is not to move on the other. Only the ancient earth holds them, understands them both. I grow pompous with love, I am solemn, I am rivering, I am avoiding the word where I began.

−36−

All the nervousness, resonance, fatuity, confusion, hope built in the word—lovers. We stuck together. That's all it means. That's all it has to mean.

−37−

A thin woman with ample young hair.

–38–

It's what we try that counts, not what pays off. Something seen, once. Again, held. Smothered in looking. So as I am with this woman, now, in all the reality as we call it of day to day starting and stopping, I am making love to that magic form, the hair I so tiresomely notice, moving ahead of me on the rock slopes as long before across the plaza. The first sight. Continuous. All activity repeats, explores, exhausts the First Sight. Then one day, acutely, suddenly, it is exhausted. What then? Then the famous *nada* of the philosophers, the stone turns back into air, the bets are off.

–39–

But not yet. I told her about it, tenderly, how bizarre it was for me to fall not for a face or a shape or some thrust of behavior out against the constraint of clothes or convention, not even for some rare walk or a torqued standing still that argued intercourse, love-lock, clinch, but for hair. It doesn't matter, she assured me, it isn't odd. It's just what what happened. It's what you happened to notice, that's all. Anything that you notice works. So naturally I wanted to know what had made her notice me. What did you notice about me, I asked. That you followed me and kept your distance.

–40–

I accepted this as definition. I am one who keeps his distance. One who follows her. Enough about me. What happened? That's all that counts, what happened? Isn't it? We, we are just the opaque solids that cast those interesting shadows called "action." Or "what happened." Don't ask me about the light that casts this shadow of us, past us, this shadow of our selves we follow all our days. Don't ask me about the light. Ask the light about itself. Ask the light.

-41-

So many days. Nights. Larches, boulders, shadows moving at the corners of the visual field—no movement when the eyes focus there. Going and stopping. Going. Staying. My kind of world—wind, rain, sun, change. We were high in the mountains, and had found a fallen-down stone hut. We took enough loose stones on the high slope to make our place habitable, even cozy on the always chilly nights. The two cars pointed their noses at the hut and were cold, quiet, out of place, reassuring to me. We had driven them as far as the road could go. Here was upland rocky pasture. Going on foot was possible. We could still go, separately or together. But we stayed.

-42-

She is washing clothes at the rushing stream, really stretching the clothes out, a few each day, and weighting them down with rocks, to let the stream bubble through them. Then she wrings them out and lets them dry all day spread on bushes. She does this every morning, and most days it works in that the cloth is dry before the inevitable late afternoon shower. In this way she keeps my own few garments clean, her own larger wardrobe rotating, full of variety, all on themes of sweater and t-shirt and slacks, though there is a grey-green woollen dress she wore one evening.

-43-

In the nighttime we kept each other warm. Enough said. These are sacred things—*favete linguis,* if you please. We ate the food stored in her car, grains mostly, and gathered mushrooms, roots and likely leaves. Neither of us cared to kill animals or fish. Sometimes we found an egg or two in a cleft on the cliff. One day we seized a partridge-like bird that a hawk had just killed on the wing and let fall. We beat the hawk off when he stooped for his prey. The partridge was good eating a day later, when we roasted it in clay—the clay hardens, and when you crack it open when you shove it out of the fire, the clay pulls away the feathers and leaves pretty clean meat. It was strange to eat a once-living thing, and to nibble at bones morphologically akin to the ones we held them by. How odd it is that people eat animals. At least we found it odd, and didn't do it again.

–44–

It was pleasant with her. We weren't accomplishing anything, but what was there to accomplish? We were the great majority, whose work is exclusively getting from here to tomorrow. We had winter to worry about, and the move it would force to lower ground, or to some solider house. I persisted in wanting to continue east. To see if anything was left there. I wasn't sure if I wanted anything to be, and voiced to her neither my wonder nor my doubting. Food would be a problem soon. As far as I was concerned, we could stay there till her trunk was empty, then hope for the best, as they say. But it was her food, and she would decide.

–45–

We played games. We imagined ourselves monarchs of just this very place, with slaves and courtiers and artisans. We planned the exact topography of court and temple, wheatfields and museums: as far as the eye could see, we mapped out our imaginary realm. No further. To see is to be. We made laws for our country, then, warming to the game of legislation, made laws for ourselves, just as we were, survivors on the mountain. We devised and enforced punishments for infractions of these new little laws. Our days flowered with fasts and silences, slaps and immobilities. Even before we got tired of these playful repressions we got a little frightened of them, to tell the truth. Hurting is so easy, so attractive. So we made laws without punishments, toothless laws, and scratched symbols that reminded us of them into nearby stones. Then we discovered that the loveliest laws are those impossible to break.

−46−

We played another game. On midnights we would sit on the hilltop and be quiet, watching the stars. Not exactly watching, just being open to them. As soon as one of us saw a shooting star, or anything else unusual (a sudden cloud, shimmer of an auroral display, satellite pass), we would turn our attention to that quarter of the sky. Each of us would pick a star and focus the mind on it, trying to receive it, imagine it, understand it. In the first phase of the game, we would simply tell each other what we'd learned. Then one night our stories were curiously similar, and after elaborate pointing up in the air, describing, measuring, quarreling and explaining, we found that we had both in fact been concentrating on the same star.

So in the second phase of the game, we'd stare at the chosen region of the sky until we could settle on some one particular point of light. Then in acting in concert we would try to connect with it—"go there" was the phrase we used. This going was silent. Only after we came back did we tell each other what we'd found. Often enough we agreed in our reports. We began to take the game more seriously, as if we had discovered science, which is, after all, just a word for knowing—knowing what there is, and knowing it in agreement with other knowers.

We learned many things about the stars, if learned is the word for it, for us. Often we would return to stars we'd visited before, to settle questions or amplify our sense of the place. Presently she began writing down what we'd discovered, naming the star with our own new names, and identifying it as well as she could by position and sightlines to obvious constellations. Our names for them, we hoped, would one day be able to be cross-referenced to orthodox star-lists if ever we came to a library again. Or met someone who remembered.

−47−

In moments of exaltation, and I am capable of them, I would think that our whole bonding, our being together at all, was destined, and destined for the sake of the Star Game and

what we were learning. I even went so far as to imagine that
these awarenesses or fantasies or whatever it is we were generat-
ing, might one day be of use to other people. That was a grand
thought, and we shared it out loud often. It made our foraging
and grubbing and eating and sleeping seem less selfish.

–48–

We took seriously too her writing down of what we discovered, and saw to it that the resultant texts were protected
from harm. They were kept in her car, wrapped in a cloth. Fresh
paper I had lots of in my car, God knows why, I'd brought several
reams of it along. And pencils. And pens. And ink. We made ink
too, from phytolacca berries, and soaked oak leaves in it, dry
orange ones, for mordant. At any rate, it made us happy, looking
at the stars, talking, telling, and the paper passing from one car
to the other, being blackened with meaning as it passed.

–49–

How did we feel about it then, when the nights were rainy?
When clouds came, we were sealed in with this single most
invisible astronomical item, the earth. We felt disappointed, im-
patient to get on with our work, which no longer had much to
do with this earth. We were, yes, thinking of it already as a
work, our work. We had other games for such dismal nights
(traveling to invented or remembered cities, naming past friends
and devising apt memorials or monuments for each), but these
remained mere games, a blend of recall and wishful thinking.
More often that not, on such nights we spent more time in sex,
and about sex, telling each other our passional histories until
each of us was jealous and huffy and thin as a piece of paper. Or
we discussed our favorite fantasies, vying with each other in
lubricity. These were breathless hours, ancient personal fixa-
tions mingling with nonce perversities improvised as we read
one another's reactions, feeding the excitement. Sometimes we
got so deeply into such revelation and confection that we'd forget we were being deprived of our stars. Once after we'd worked

each other up and tumbled into love and drifted off to sleep, I woke abruptly to step outside. The wind was up, and had wiped the sky clean. The stars were all there, and I felt ashamed of myself for being alone beneath them, untravelling, irresponsible, exhausted.

–50–

During the day we would usually read back over everything she had written down. The reading took form and pleasure from the world of speculative learning it recorded. It gestured back at the reports we'd made, as the reports gestured back to the 'travelling.' But as days passed, I would sometimes come across passages registering reports or adventures I did not remember. I've never had much confidence in my personal memory, so these New Topics (as we later thought of them) did not much surprise me. Still, there grew in me an uneasiness or suspicion that some things had come into being in the very act of writing, and referenced nothing outside themselves. This was a disquieting thought, but an exciting one as well. I never was able to be sure, one way or the other, whether writing did indeed at times generate meaning rather than record it. What would it be like to read without remembering?

–51–

What would it be like if one read what one wrote, really read it? And built a circle of objection around it, and a new synthesis around that, then an outer ring of objectivity, and a river of feeling around that, and so kept on building, ever more accurate and more perspicuous, more honest and more generous, out to the edges of one's thought, and then, impelled by the sheer habit of building, found oneself thinking well beyond the edges of one's thinking, circles of intellection and faithful reflection, on and on, into the beautiful blue distances of contradiction, under the clean wind of qualification, the sun shining? Isn't that the famous city of Deioces we read about in Herodotus, a pure crystal built out from the seed of the First Thought, the original quick insight that years later looks like the center? What a school it would be to embroil our own Best Thoughts in an urgent conscientious scarcely-ending structure of our own Best Thinking. No one can ever think a thought he isn't smart enough to contradict. And then see through the contradiction, and qualify that new perception with yet sharper thinking, which in its turn is susceptible, immediately, to contradiction, then qualification, restatement, leading to new perception, new thinking. We have the tools to turn our opinions and insights into thinking. But by clinging to what-I-thought and what-I-mean, we are kept busy in rhetoric, hired mouthpieces defending some paltry *but I meant* ... We have invested in polemics and persuasions, raised a standing army to protect a city we never get around to building. Do it. Build the starry terraces and the deep reflecting moats, the subtle walls and lucid gates. A thought is only worth its own contradiction. Contradict yourself.

–52–

I always think there is a chance. No matter how bad the situation. If I were falling down the sheer north face of Jo-mo Lung-ma in the high mountains we seem to be heading towards, eight thousand feet straight drop, I still would think I had a chance. It's the way I'm made. It makes me seem less than serious, though I am very serious. It makes tragedy a less than available form for me. So the prospect of winter and starvation did not unduly alarm me, certainly not to the borders of funk. It did bother her, especially now she thought she was pregnant. At the time, we didn't realize how few people were getting pregnant, and didn't know how lucky we were. It just seemed locally terrible, a fate, a constriction of our movements (what movements?), a question (Human Liberty) too quickly answered (Human Life).

-53-

I could hardly see it straight, much less say it. Her hair, my hurry. The truth: when we thought she was pregnant (we were pregnant), what I really felt was fear, jabbering dry-mouthed fear. Anything else I said or showed was swagger. What I felt was fear, and I can't tell what she felt because my fear was screaming too loud. I longed for her menstrual blood to flow; it would heal me like Jordan.

-54-

What will we do for a house?
    Light the small air with a bird.
What will we eat?
    The shadows of flags flapping on the mountainside.

What flags? We had come to a region which seemed still inhabited. One day we were out foraging east, further than we had ventured before, a warmer day than we'd had for weeks. We were finding some good things and caching them safe on the trail, to pick up on the way back to the hut. We were on a steep slope, cold in shadow there, when we heard a curious sound, familiar, hard to name, coming from the other side of the crest. We clambered up to peer down. Below, on a far gentler slope, five black tents were pitched, and from their guy ropes many small flags, triangular, were flapping in the smart breeze. Their fluttering made the sound we heard.

We crept back down and retreated to our place, gathering the stowed fruits and roots along the way. Only when we were safe home did we dare to discuss what we had seen. Tents suggested nomads, the flags gave a settled air, as if they were flying to protect the campsite, as if those who camped there gave some care to the land. We decided that whoever they were, they would stay a while longer, so we could afford to think a while, and see how things felt, and maybe pay another furtive visit near dawn or dusk. Did we want to make contact?

Then she wrote a poem of sorts on one of the star pages, in the margin, as it stands at the head of this section. It was the first thing written apart from the star travel research reports.

–55–

In dream the flapping little flags recurred, white, green, red, yellow, blue—most of them faded, a few fresh, intense even against the stiff blue sky.

But of course when we did go back, after days of endless talk about it and our readiness for expanding our circle of acquaintance, days of rehearsal and doubt, the black tents were away and their flags gone.

She and I had no kind of mountain savvy, so we could not read the signs, if any, that would explain who those people were, and where they'd gone. She picked up on the hillside a few stones with painted symbols on them, looked like writing we could not read, letters of several colors, curved and fringed, like flags flaunting. She soon found herself writing a lot about flags fluttering, and birds flapping, and black houses that move in the night. And blood, lots about blood. It made her happy, evidently, but it seemed to me it took away, this writing or poetry of hers, some of the keenness of her involvement in our star researches. I didn't much like the feeling of jealousy in me, so for some days I thought of the star game as just a game, and didn't do it much. But secretly I missed it, the seriousness of it.

–56–

Evidently I was getting bored with our life on the mountain, so I was pleased one day when she read me a piece asking how flags on earth were like stars in heaven, comparison, and seemed to guess the latter more interesting than the former. I took it that she was coyly, even obscurely, signaling her own desire to resume our researches. I concealed my satisfaction, as I had my distress, and that night we played our game ardently again, and told each other great things we had learned beyond the stars. And once more the nights passed well.

-57-

I still didn't like this we. I'm back to that. All these mountains, hawks, wolves, marmots, clouds, nomads, winds roving
free, and there I was, trapped in a pronoun. Trapped in her hair.
Not in her hair. Trapped in the original day, hour, when I first
perceived her hair. Caught in an old perception. Why did I feel
trapped? How did she feel? Ask her. Ask yourself what it must
be like to be living with me. With such as me. With? In a hut.
On a mountain. In the world.

-58-

Of course I knew things. Or there were things I knew. I
knew there were likely to be gods behind appearances, or rather
that behind the appearance of the world there were the appearances of gods and other beings. I mean that this very world, seen
as we usually see it, was in fact (or in deeper seeming) a vaster
and more beautiful world if we saw it better. To see this not as
that, but as the truest this. Not a different world. This. This. It
seemed important that I knew this. In the daytime I told her
about it, and she neither argued nor assented. One night I rea-
soned out loud that what we were seeing or intuiting in the stars
was really right here, seeing this world rightly, for a change. No,
she said. No, it might be like that, but it isn't. It's really different. The stars are the stars.

-59-

But I didn't know what she knew, only what she said and
what she did. I'm the kind who always thinks there's something
else. A rat behind the arras. Rats aplenty on this mountain,
tawny and beige ones, big. My mind, any mind, a thing that
loops from thing to thing. This hopping is called thinking.
Mind's a hopper—good word, because that's also a thing where
things are stored ready for delivery. Out the chute. Out the
mouth. Mind a hopper—I'd call it a monkey but there are no
monkeys on this mountain. Musk-deer and bear and wolves and

lynxes and rock rats, and the mind hopping all day long until it hops behind the curtain at night and we call ourselves asleep. Even then the hopping goes on and on, in a place so strange, or at least so dark, that later neither the mouth nor the head can make much of it.

–60–

So to my way of thinking, what she knew would be the sum of all the trajectories of her hops, and where her trajectories intersected mine we would have the condition, though certainly not the act, called Communication in the old days. It is hard to be with another person. It is hard. It's hard to be a person to begin with, it is hard to do anything. We never talked about this. We talked about the cloud terraces of Aldebaran and so forth, not about this. This isn't a this, not to talk about, really. Not really.

–61–

Sometimes I wished I had known her, or almost known her, in the old days, in a city. I could have stared at her below purple and cobalt stained glass windows in a hot café, danced at her in a disco, talked at her in a busy noonday park beneath a traffic-dizzy gingko tree. We could have known each other lightly, glancing caresses, gentle recoils. I'm not sure that I'm all that worth knowing, the way she had to know me now, there being no one else around to know. Still, we could have gone on, alone or together, there were others, out there. Had to be. There are always other people.

–62–

How certain we can be when no one is listening. I can swear the rock into my conspiracy of meaning, and count on the cloud to assent to my opinions by giving its sign of passing by over-head. The world is not full of signs—the world is nothing but signs. To notice anything at all, let alone talk of it, is to ensnare myself in a web of interpretation. Some mornings I would wake and nuzzle into her rich hair, and rest my hand on her breast, whose nipple would rise to graze the hollow of my palm as if we were always new. I would count her gentle breaths until I fell asleep again.

—63—

For all the mountain air and Arcady, we were not early risers. The star game kept us up late, and she would jot down notes and reminders of our talk, by firelight, to work up into clear narrative next day. So next day might start as late as noon. Myself, I loved the dawntime, and that's when I'd often wake a while, even walk up or down our hill and guess the coming weather. It seemed tame compared to our stars, but I could do it alone. A white walk at morning, as if I believed in something. Sign of health: I believe in what I make up. Sign of sickness: not very strongly. I keep believing the day. I take it back with me and breathe it in her hair.

—64—

The nomads are back, decent people who lead goats, or are led by them. They had been to a religious festival celebrated with drunkenness and astrological calculations from which they're still dizzy. They call themselves Sog-po, and a few of them speak our language. Their culture was very little influenced by the world below the mountains, and very little changed by the squalid endings the rest of us had been witnessing, contriving, suffering in that world of plains and ships and coasts.

They found us. We came out one morning and saw their tents, eight now, being set up silently all round us. They were looking at our cars without much interest, certainly less than the goats showed, one of whom was chewing my left rear tire.

–65–

These people seem to take it for granted that we will go on travelling with them, simply join their band. I don't know what to make of this menacing hospitality. I feel their kindness as a blow, a wound in the intimacy she and I had inhabited. The same boring intimacy I now felt so precious.

–66–

It is a long time since I've shaved. My beard, at first as bristly as the beak of a crow, has filled out and turned softer, though still rough on her skin. Her chin. My beard already has a wildness in it that feels under my hand the way her hair looks to my eyes. Maybe I'm about to turn into her, in my own way. Maybe I've looked too much at her hair. Taken it as a constant sign, telling me why I am here.

–67–

The Sog-po are pretty impressed by my beard, and laugh about it a lot. They themselves can barely grow a few wisps on lip and chin. But her hair seemed to mean little to them. How odd its color must be to them, the tawniness must seem to them animal, not human. Humans have black hair. Except the Buddha, they tell me, whose hair they paint blue.

–68–

Apart from beard and hair, she and I managed to keep ourselves looking civil, even clean. Washing was getting harder, not just because the nomads were curious and uninhibited in their interests. Morning and night were cold now; more and more we bathed at noon while the nomads were at their lunch. Or on windless days when the rocks late afternoon gave back the warmth they've been storing all the day. At noon, water behaves differently from any other time. It takes the light in, and plays with it deeply. Not the surface filigree we see at sunset, the sheens and satins and lacework, but some deep musical stirring down there, of which we, shivering babblers, lip up only the furthest froth, rinse our mouths and snort water from our noses like young horses in the sun.

–69–

She was leaving me. That was clear. I had explored her needs with what delicacy I could, and refused to make the sort of claims she needed me to make so she could feel truly linked to me. It is not, apparently, enough to be together. I knew it would be like this, one or the other would withdraw, with the usual dead weight of grief, hurt, you name it, left behind. I was a little surprised that it wasn't my move, that I didn't leave her—I'm such a good leaver.

–70–

Or was it me after all? I could feel the going ripening in her. But it didn't have to be away from me. It was I who by understanding it so could make it so. This tribe of goatherds, these greasy comrades, offered us a society into which our own intimacy would be poured, lost like a glass of water in a river. To go with her among others—this was to go from her. Why did I make it so? Was my whole sense of her imminent departure funded only by my own intention to depart, or by my awareness that I could sustain a relationship only in the absurd vacuum of a two-person world?

Where will the stars be when we are not alone together? I asked her. The self-pitying words of my question weaseled, but she understood. We have to go on—we can't be alone anymore, winter is real. But the stars will be brighter still then, and we can be alone with them still.

–71–

Our staple food was gone now. We were on our last bag of barley. If we tried to go it alone, as I was still inclined to do, jealously preserving our enforced intimacy, we would have to start eating animals. We tried to talk about it, mounted a practical discussion of what it would be like to catch, kill, skin, disembowel, clean and cook one of the gorgeously cute fat furry marmots so frequent on our mountain. I thought of the yellow fat under its fur, I thought of intestines full of alien shit. I thought of the sheer blood of the thing. We gave up thinking about it. We knew that if hunger drove us, we'd wind up doing it, we could do it, catch it and kill it and eat it. What we could not do was think about it.

–72–

All the while the Sog-po were giving us milk and cheese and yogurt, bread made from barley they'd bartered for, god knows where. Every meal we accepted from these cheerful givers enrolled us more deeply into their tribe, into their future moves. Already I took my turn watching goats on the hill, when I could be bothered. Already she worked at the churn, giggling while the ladies howled as the milk sloshed up all over her thighs from her awkward plunges.

–73–

It was hard for us to find time to be alone together. Even though we had not moved a mile from our hut, and slept together every night, the going was on us. Just to be alone we would stroll out to gather medicinal plants on the steeper slopes, before the greedy goats omnivored the rocks bare. One day we found, or noticed at last, a clump of low herbs growing in sun only a furlong or so from our hut. We imagined it, from the smell and my fondness for the name, to be one of the labiatae. The stem, nibbled, gave a minty taste, and the leaf was warm in the lips, like basil. We trimmed several plants and filled her t-shirt, held scooped out before her like an apron. At home we made tea of some of the leaves, and while it brewed, I ground some leaves into a fine glowing oily emerald sludge, and mixed it into the cold barley porridge saved from breakfast. The taste was good, but made our lack of salt more evident. She had brought only a small vial of some vegetable salt substitute with her, motivated by a post-civilized food fad (foods that humans have eaten for ten thousand years are bad for you). We had finished it weeks before. The nomads, so generous in other things, were stingy with their little leathern pouches of salt. How can you make love without salt?

–74–

Tea and green porridge, saltless, our evening meal. In the last light, digesting, I looked down and saw that a little green sauce had sprung from my rock quern and stained my wrist. Later, in full dark, I was to find precisely this green mark among the stars, an intense emerald star in Scorpio. She went there with me, without any need to discussing our target. Our reports were copious and congruent. It took her two hours next morning to write down the full account.

–75–

But before that dark, before that star, we sat with our tea and looked down the hill. I felt intensely languid, the way I used rarely to feel when, a smoker in those days, I wanted a cigarette but felt too lazy (no, not lazy—something else, still, quiet, contained) to reach into my own shirt pocket to get one. Sometimes my own hands are the furthest things in the world.

–76–

What was this tea? Why do things have effects? What does it mean to be hungry, hungry all the time until you're not? This curious pale tea, was it having some psychic effect? What am I talking about—everything taken into the body is a drug, everything has an effect, every effect is psychic. What else are we? We are consequences of lettuce and air. The mysteries of cabbage solve themselves in us. We were stoned, that's what we were. But we were always stoned, confused effects who loved each other strongly. Or wrongly, as if we were causes.

–77–

The nomads had declined our offers of the tea, and watched us carefully after we took it. Next day they smiled a lot, and found it especially funny that she had so much to write down in her book. They had books of their own, old ones, and some of them could read in them. They found it hilarious that we were writing a book—books for them were uncreated, timeless, authentic, given. They looked at our activities with the affectionate amusement of parents whose child waves his toy shovel and says Look, Mommy, I'm building a mountain!

When we tried to share the results of our star researches with them, however, they were interested enough, asked questions, proposed agreements and demurrals, much as if we were all talking about the same world.

So in the midst of all our going away from each other, we also found this bound or limit which turned us back in toward each other.

–78–

We knew the risks, then, of what we had to do. It was a decent thing, an ancient thing, finding salt, like keeping warm in winter. Every step we took to find it would recruit us to the army of humanity, mammality, that from the start of life has been marching and scheming and trading and taxing for its salt. Conceding our need for salt was like being pregnant—it was an unimpeachable avowal of our confederacy with nature.

We would go with these people who were kind and who at least respected our union. We would leave the cars behind; though they had some life left in their reactors, there were no roads eastward. Someday someone might want them, to go back down there, where things began and ended. Not us. We had to do our living gracefully now, like all the poor, going on foot where there was to go. And we both knew, we all know, that to find salt you have to approach on foot, humbly expecting nothing and asking nothing but to survive. Humbly, the way people look for other people.

−79−

"We have to gather," she said. From our observations of stars and what went on in their planets, I had a sense of what she meant. By being together so long, we had been gathered. The bond between us, still never discussed, possessed definite physical force now—we had seen this in those other places out there—by which other people could be connected to us, spurs or perpendiculars to our link, a weft to our given warp. We could weave. We could help them to be.

−80−

To gather means to weave, to take one's place (our place) in the web of continuity made up of all such gatherings. This is a doctrine without divorce. Every departure is a right-angled turn onto another line of the same texture. You can't escape, but you can't get lost. We could gather, therefore we must gather. Our link would make cities happen. New ones, built of strong invisible bonds between all the weak people we were.

−81−

And so I went on waking up in her hair. I loved to be there because I didn't know anything. Or anything but that. We had no soaps any more, but we were clean, clean as the stream made us. We walked with the people around us. Nothing had to be decided. And as soon as I knew that, everything was decided.

5

The Irish Joke

*An Irishman by chance stepped out of his house
and left some cooking on the stove. As he closed the
door behind him, the wind blew out the flame and
gas began to fill the kitchen. When the man came
back in, he struck a match to light his pipe. Instantly
the room exploded and the Irishman was hurled
through the roof and into the branches of a great oak
nearby.*

*As he clung dazed to the branch, he looked down
and saw his house had burst into flames and was
being consumed.*

*Just then, his neighbor came hurrying up, and
cried out to him, "McEnteggart, you poor soul, what a
terrible thing it is!"*

*McEnteggart looked down from the tree and said,
"I'm just thanking God I got out before the fire
started!"*

This is an Irish joke, told to me by my father, who (thanks
to his name, I suppose) thinks of himself as Irish, and hence
permitted to say such stuff. I grasp the same permission.

It is Irish because it makes good seem to arise out of evil. It
is Irish because, to begin with, the poor fool blows out his flame,
pays too little attention (that taxation of the mind), destroys his
house and health for the sake of a smoke. It is Irish because
nothing goes right with him, yet there he is, happy as a kite in a
tree, with words in his mouth to say for himself. What more can
he want?

Men are birds and birds are men, a tree is a fitting repose for a wandering scholar like himself, McEnteggart (I call him that because the name means Son of the Priest, scion of the theological-industrial establishment that has run old Ireland all these years). In his tree he looks about him and looks down at this roaring ruin that five minutes ago had been his own dear wee house, and all he can see is something to be happy about, something to talk about. God, is there never an end to Irish palaver? The beauty of it, fresh bread in the oven and warm milk in the pail are not in it compared to talk, talk, talk. The lovely man, in his tree, the still unlit pipe still gripped in his decayed teeth, not a light for it and all that fire down there, his beer and his Bible going up as smoke into the pale nostrils of the day.

Ah, what will I do with McEnteggart? I want to cry when I think of him up there, and at any moment his grasp might weaken and he might fall. I think of his loss and his discomfiture, and why isn't that gabby neighbor busy fetching a ladder or the fire brigade. Why does he stand looking up into the tree and talking? Why doesn't McEnteggart tell him to do something useful? Because nothing is to be done. As long as he can talk he can work, and as long as he can work he can hold up his head amidst his fellows, and what need has a man for more than that?

I feel so bad about him, losing his house like that. I surely wouldn't want to lose mine. And though I don't smoke and my stove is electric, the curse of Inattentiveness has its pallid mark on me too. And even past any derelictions of my own, there is always the gnawing mouse, the frayed wire, the down-forking lightning, the oilcan exploding by the burner. There is the furtive vengeful arsonist whom long ago I chanced to offend. If I laugh at McEnteggart, am I not more likely to share some version of his fate?

I don't know. That is an Irish question, and an Irish answer. He is in the tree and he has his own species of gratitude to stand between him and the immensity of his loss. Or maybe it matters less to him than it would to me.

I Wanted a Fugue

In my simplicity I wanted a fugue, what could be better, a lightfall shifting and shaping of the substance-in-form, *gZugs*, on the flaggy premise that whatever meaning anything had could arise only from its interaction with (a) itself again and again, and (b) something reminiscent of itself but clearly other. Two different melodies. Two different men. Gender differences within a species. Insolvency of touch. Or does touch one day utterly avail, utterly? This other thing, twisting around. A twenty dollar bill crumpled in a back pocket, alone with the cloth and the buttock. I wanted it, but not in any simple way, though it is always good to hear. Good to hear. Fugue, starting with simple subjects, two things at one time, leading to the essence, all things at one time, until at the end of the world you hear it, what all music is about, the quintessence itself: one thing at one time. Art starts. Caves full of magnitudes. Semiotics of randomness. I drowsed on the ashlar above the waterfall, amazing black the water was, how easy I could fall in, black, save where creamy Irish lace stirred round before fading back, into the glossy black. The way things fade into themselves. How surprising it always is when a child becomes a woman. That it never stops. That is the flight of it, the flurry of its name. My name. *Fuga*, delusional, sortie from the consensus. Hurrying toward—?

How cold it is here under the pines, by the bank of again the Mill River where it divides the park (Look) just as it divided the town (Leeds) from the country club's greens. Cold English water headed swiftly south towards the ox-bow where it joins the Connecticut and becomes American for that last hundred miles or so before it becomes the world, just worldly, the Sound, Great

Ocean. The fugue specifies gender differences and four ways of walking—

Downtown, Uptown, Upside Down and Inside Out—Fux's treatise tells a version of this story, back when cherries were red and only bishops were gay. The red sun, getting ready for a colder evening than we've had in days divests itself of ruddiness. Barely yellower, then polished silver oddly like the pale blue sky it sinks through towards the pines that crest the little rise the river snakes around between my love's house and where I sit cold-fingered spinet-less dithering of fugues.

Hypnogeography

West of Ninth Avenue the high bluff ends; the land falls away abruptly in a series of cliffs and steep hillsides canted just enough to bear grass among the pale scars where rivulets have scored the earth on their way down to the Hudson. To get there, they must cross the long grassy meadows along the river, the very fertile alluvial tract that stretches north the whole length of the island. Winding streams get there gently, and smooth, unbordered roads wander here and there, past small, neat farmsteads, taverns and gas stations. The light is sea-light everywhere, and clouds bank richly, picturesquely, over the dark Jersey palisades. When it rains, the rain comes sweeping in from the west, angular as autumn sunlight at dusk on golden Sundays. But when the sun shines it is sweet and steady, coming evenly down like a decent teacher in grammar school, fair to all her pupils. I like to walk around here, or drive the little roadster you can rent at almost any garage. The roads aren't paved, and we New Yorkers like it that way. This is farm country, and from its good black soil most of what we put on our plates is grown.

East of the cliffs, though, the city gets busy. Tall white buildings everywhere, hundreds of thousands of them cunningly nestled close together without each denying another's light. Crowded as can be, but the streets don't seem that way. In fact I find it strange how empty they usually are, considering how densely built up every block is now. The banks are beautiful, and there are fountains in front of the meanest church. I'm fond of the lower East 30s and upper 20s, where small townhouses manage to skulk unbothered between clubs and foundations and sleek hotels operated by people who say they come from North-

175

ern Italy. The north side of Canal Street is lined with shops and restaurants facing the canal. People sit outside to watch the little skiffs and sculls nip along the broad water. But south of Canal, the land is more open, with broad fields and a good deal of woodland, little woods on low hilltops, and hardly any buildings. The dirt roads are dusty in the summer time, but vacationers revelling in the wine gardens and outdoor theaters and ball courts don't mind. In the shade of a big cottonwood I leaned on somebody's mailbox and watched a young woman get out of her car and go into the courtyard of an inn across the way. The wind fluffed out the tulle of her dress and I heard it sigh against her legs. How quiet it is here, and the wind itself needs us to make enough resistance for it to be heard.

This is how it is in my dreams. I mean real dreams, the kind you have at night when you leave your mind and body alone a while. For years I have been having dreams in which I walk around New York City, where I was born, and where I lived for the first 25 years of this life. The New York I dream in is a little different from what I see when I go there by train now, and some aspects of the dream New York is what I have just been describing.

It is not New York before modern times—-cars run around, big Late Capitalism buildings abound in the denser parts of town. It is, as far as I know, not New York after some implausible reconstruction after some all too likely disaster. It is just New York as it is, exactly as it is, in dream.

So what I want to know is this: all over the earth women and men are dreaming every night, and among all their other dreams of love and terror and monsters and mates, they have dreams of place. I want to know the places they dream. I have a feeling that the Dream Representation of place can tell us a lot about what we think of as the 'real' place. Smart people like the Highland Maya of Guatemala (I'm relying on what Dennis Tedlock told me once) are concerned not just with what a person looks like or does for a living, but how he 'represents' in dream. I want to learn, and want us to learn, how our countries and cities represent in dream.

With that in mind, I want there to be a science or a study. I have given it the name Hypnogeography just because everybody can figure that out.

What I propose is that all generous persons record their dreams [in general a good thing to do] when they dream of place, and that the records or recitations of these dreams be collected, examined, compared—that is, compared with one another and, when possible, with the undreamt 'real' place we find at the end of the road in from the airport.

When all such dreams have been assembled and overlaid, a truer geography will appear. I don't mean that the Dream Place is truer than the so-called 'real,' but that all versions of a place are needed to know the Place most truly. That's the goal, and this is the project I have in mind. And the mind is what we finally get to know, as dearly in need of mapping as any virus or nucleic acid strand. And how to map the mind, except by what we tell each other?

This statement was read 10 September 1986 to the Hudson Celebration at the Omega Institute, Rhinebeck, New York

The Closet

People who are hard to find make it hard for other people. Other people have enough trouble, what with making it hard for themselves. It all is difficult, isn't it. This unripe fruit of what we mean. Of what we want. When is the thing going to ripen like a dress falling to the floor in the dark closet? Inside the rind it is as soft and dark as in a closet.

Children enjoy the smelly soft clothes that brush over their foreheads and shoulders as they crouch. Wherever you live you have to find the local jungle and be there. You can only be anything like free when you find the jungle and sit down in it, sink in it, get lost in it, drown in trees. So little light comes down.

Children don't need light all that much, just for growing, not for being. They're afraid of the dark because they're in the dark and they have a good sense of who they are already. Stop being so fucking afraid of yourself, he told her. Your doubts bore me.

Imagine sitting in a closet on the floor under all the dresses and overcoats and neatly creased trousers upside down, cuffs nipped in their squeeze hangers, and belts and ties and scarves that slip off their hooks when you lean against the back wall and slide down until you're sitting on the floor. You're sitting on the floor with your knees up and you light a match.

A single match. You carried it in with you and now its wood is damp and a little soft from your sweaty hand. You are afraid it is too damp to light. You scrape it on the floor between your legs and it bursts into noisy flame. How loud light is. The light is enough for you to see everything in the closet, but you don't want to use the light for that, you know what's there, your family's clothes, and you're not interested in them. You want to see the fire. You want to use the flame to see itself.

You watch it burn, your fingers deftly turning the match so the flame burns up the shaft slowly. You pinch the very end of the wood so the flame can burn as long as it can. It burns your fingers before it goes out, and the little pain that comes from that is pleasant, a prolongation of the glow, a translation of fire into a different medium, into your body.

As long as you can feel the pain, the fire is still somewhere. In a few seconds that too is gone and the bright spot left in your eyes is fading through its successive colors, shifting around the visual field as your eyes roam unseeing around the lifeless geometry of the closet. Outside the closet door they are probably looking for you. Where is she now? Why is she always so hard to find?

Invitation

What I ask is the opportunity to meet with you on a platform overlooking some grass of ordinary greenness. No band need be playing, but if one is, let it operate the sort of music our grandparents understood as light classical: Waldteufel, Suppé, Ippolitov-Ivanov. Things turn into other things all round us; Chinese conjurors elicit curious ribbons of light from the sky in many colors; these they braid or spool together, and sell, hanks of sunshine, to women in the crowd. We look down, and I wonder out loud if they really are Chinese . . . Han? not Han? You urge me to pay less attention to my doubts, my scruples, and more to my fantasies. "In this great wheel," you say, "a wonder sleeps. If you don't rouse it, you can live its dream all your life." I am grateful to you, less for that reinforcement than for being here with me. You could easily be with someone else, or even more readily alone. But you bear me company, and allow your right foot to tap beside my left. Tap to the music, since that still goes on. Indefatigable arm of the conductor!